A CHRISTMAS HOMECOMING

Anne Perry

headline

First published in 2011 by
HEADLINE PUBLISHING GROUP

First published in paperback in 2012 by
HEADLINE PUBLISHING GROUP

1

Cataloguing in Publication Data is available from the British Library

ISBN 978 0 7553 7694 0

Typeset in TimesNewRomanPS by Palimpsest Book Production Limited,
Falkirk, Stirlingshire

Printed and bound in Great Britain by
Clays Ltd, St Ives plc

Headline's policy is to use papers that are natural, renewable and recyclable products and
made from wood grown in sustainable forests. The logging and manufacturing processes
are expected to conform to the environmental regulations of the country of origin.

HEADLINE PUBLISHING GROUP
An Hachette UK Company
338 Euston Road
London NW1 3BH

www.headline.co.uk
www.hachette.co.uk

To those who face the unknown with courage

Caroline Fielding saw the huge mansion rising from the steep incline ahead of them as the carriage turned the corner, and felt an almost overwhelming sense of relief. It was the end of a very long journey and she was aching with tiredness and from the biting cold. First there had been the early morning ride to the station in London. The platforms had been crowded and it had been difficult for her and Joshua to push their way through with all the luggage, trying not to bump into people. She had been glad to find their seats for the journey to York.

In York they had disembarked. One piece of luggage had been mislayed and as time was short they were desperate to find it. She had asked the same porter the same questions over and over, until at last it was safely stowed in the guards' van on the train to Whitby. Then she and Joshua had almost run along the platform as carriage doors clanged shut and the engine belched steam and smuts, and they scrambled in just as the train began to move.

Now in the dark, and with newly fallen snow, they rode

in a two-horse carriage from Whitby up to the cliff edge and this house where they would spend the whole Christmas holiday, if you could call it a holiday.

She turned to look at Joshua beside her. Aware of her movement, he touched her gloved hand lightly.

'A bit brooding, isn't it?' he said ruefully. 'But I expect it'll be warm inside, and we'll be very welcome.'

The coach lamps did not give enough light to see his face, but she could imagine it: gentle, mercurial, full of humour. She heard the half-apology in his voice.

'It'll be excellent,' she said without hesitation. She would never be as good an actor as he was, because she was always herself, and it was his profession to imagine himself inside another man's skin, even his heart. But she had long ago learned to mask her feelings for the sake of those she loved, and she did love him. However, there were fears that crowded her every so often because she was so much older than he, and she did not belong to the theatre as he did. She feared she would always be an outsider, too old for him in the eyes of his fellows, too ordinary, undramatic and painfully respectable. Yet she would have been wretched had she given in to conventionality and remained a widow after her first husband's death. And how could she have married anyone else when she loved Joshua so much? She felt no inner doubt or shadow about her second marriage although outwardly it had not been at all the right thing to do.

For a moment Joshua's hand tightened over hers.

They climbed the last hundred yards of the road, horses

straining against the weight of the vehicle, and finally pulled to a stop in front of the magnificent entrance of the mansion. The doors were flung open, flooding the portico and the gravel driveway with light.

'You are right,' Caroline said with a smile. 'We are welcome.'

A footman opened the door and Joshua climbed out quickly, turning to assist Caroline. She had been glad of the cloak and her huge skirts while on the journey – they provided the only warmth available – but now they were an encumbrance as she tried to step down elegantly. She grasped Joshua's hand rather more firmly than she had intended, and stood up straight to her full height just as their host, Charles Netheridge, came out of his ostentatious front door. He descended the wide steps, holding out his hand.

Introductions were made and orders given. Footmen materialised to unpack the boxes and trunks, and see to the horses.

Charles Netheridge was a stocky man, thick-chested, heavy-shouldered. His grey hair was still strong, but receding a little at the front as he moved into his sixties. In the flare of the outside lights, his features were blunt and vigorous, as was his manner. His father had made a fortune in coal. Charles had augmented it and later also built up his wealth in jet. It was his pleasure to donate generously to the theatre in London and to know that some of the best performances would never have found an audience without his intervention.

Now he had one of England's most dynamic actors in his own home, and he was brimming over with satisfaction. He led his guests inside, calling out orders for their comfort,

3

refreshment, for luggage to be taken to their rooms, and everything done for their wellbeing.

Caroline barely had time to glance around the hall, with its grey and white marble floor and its high ceiling from which hung a splendid chandelier. The warmth enveloped her and just now that was all she cared about.

'Mr Singer is already here,' Netheridge said cheerfully. 'He told me he is to play the hero, Van Helsing.' He looked a little self-conscious as he said this last, looking earnestly at Joshua as if trying to read his thoughts.

Joshua composed his expression in a manner Caroline had come to understand. He was concealing a very considerable irritation.

'I think he will be,' he agreed. 'But we will make no final decisions until we have read through Miss Netheridge's dramatisation.'

'Of course, of course,' Netheridge agreed. 'All in good time. I hope Mr Hobbs and Miss Carstairs, and Miss Rye will get here before too long. It's a nasty night, and set to get worse, I think. No doubt we'll have a good deal of snow by Christmas. Seven days to go before the performance.' He looked at Joshua narrowly, a steady, curiously unblinking stare. 'Long enough for you to get it right, do you think? No idea if it's any good. Alice has no experience, you know.'

Joshua made himself smile. 'You'll be surprised how quickly it'll come.'

'Damn silly story, if you ask me,' Netheridge murmured, half to himself. 'Vampires, indeed! But it seems to be all the rage in London, or so they say. Who is this fellow Bram Stoker? What kind of a name is "Bram"?'

'Short for Abraham,' Joshua replied.

Netheridge looked at him wide-eyed. 'Jewish?'

'I'm told he's Irish,' Joshua said with a brief smile, but Caroline saw the slight stiffening of his body and the tension in his shoulders. She had learned not to leap to his defence: to do so was patronising, as if there were something about being Jewish that needed explaining. But it was difficult for her. It is instinctive to protect those whom we love; and the more open to hurt they are, the fiercer our retaliation.

Netheridge did not even appear to be aware that he had been clumsy. This was not the time to let him know. They needed him in the new year of 1898. Without his support their next play would not open. In return for that, Joshua and the lead actors in his company were going to spend eight days over Christmas as Netheridge's guests, and perform his daughter's amateur dramatisation of Stoker's new novel, *Dracula*. In the book, the storm had washed ashore the coffin with the vampire inside it at Whitby. Alice Netheridge's play would be performed on Boxing Day, the day after Christmas, for an audience of Netheridge's friends and neighbours.

Eliza Netheridge came hurrying out of the passage at the back of the hall. She was a small woman, whose fair hair was going grey and in whose gentle face her strength was not immediately apparent. Now she looked concerned as her husband made the introductions with a touch of impatience, as if he thought she should already have been there.

'You must be tired,' Eliza said warmly, looking first at Caroline, then at Joshua. 'And cold. I'm sure you would like to go to your room and rest a little before dinner.'

'Thank you,' Caroline accepted quickly. 'That is most kind. It has been rather a long journey, and we very much wish to be at our best tomorrow.'

'Of course,' Eliza smiled. 'Will dinner at eight be suitable to you? We can always serve you something in the breakfast room at a different time, if you wish?'

'Eight will be excellent,' Caroline assured her, starting to walk towards the stairs.

The bedroom they were shown to was large and richly curtained in dark wine red. There were chairs near the fire, which spread such a light and a warmth that it was unnecessary to use the candles except on the bedside table.

Joshua stood in the middle of the room as soon as the door was closed behind the footman who had brought their cases.

'I told you,' he said gently. 'We are very welcome.' He was smiling, although his face, which reflected emotion so easily, could not hide either his weariness or a degree of anxiety.

Caroline walked over to stand close to him, then reached forward and touched his cheek softly with her fingertips. 'Don't worry about it tonight, my dear. You'll all work on the play tomorrow, and it may not be nearly as difficult when you rehearse it together as it seems now on the page. How often have you told me that about other plays?'

He leaned forward and kissed her. 'Actually it's awful,' he said ruefully. 'It's a very difficult thing to adapt a book for the stage, and Alice Netheridge really hasn't much idea. I wouldn't even attempt this if we weren't at our wits' end to find a backer for next year. But without Netheridge's support we would all be facing a pretty bleak spring.'

'That's not true, Joshua,' she corrected him. 'The company would, but you could always find a part somewhere. I know of at least three other managers who would leap at the chance to have you.'

He winced very slightly; it was just a tightening of the skin across the bones of his cheeks. 'Walk away and leave the rest of the company with nothing?' he asked. 'The theatre is too small a world to do that, even if I were willing to. It's not only Mercy and James, or Lydia – not to mention Vincent; although he would probably find something else. It's all the others as well; the bit players who do a dozen other things: moving scenery, fetching and carrying, building props, looking after the costumes.'

She had known he would say something like that, but when he did it still gave her a rush of warmth beyond the reach of the fire.

He was frowing a little. 'Are you afraid?' he asked. She had been used to being provided for, more than adequately, all her life. First it had been by her father, then Edward Ellison. This was the first time she had ever realised, more than in theory, that it was possible she could become cold or hungry, or truly frightened of debt, afraid of a knock on the door. Should she lie? Was honesty between them worth more than courage, or kindness? Which was the greater kindness anyway?

'Not yet,' she said with a tiny grimace. 'Just don't expect too much from Alice Netheridge. Can you steer some sort of path between her work as it stands, and what you would consider good enough professionally?'

'Between the rocks and the whirlpool?' He said it with a twisted smile, but there was no laughter in his eyes. 'I can try. And keep Vincent from taking over and hogging the stage, Lydia from giving up altogether, and Mercy and James from endlessly defending each other from attacks that no one has made, while at the same time teaching Alice Netheridge how to do all the extra parts, and play a credible Count Dracula myself?' He shrugged. 'Of course. My wife overrates me perhaps, but she thinks I can.' His voice dropped a little. 'At least she says so.'

Dinner was a very generous affair, but informal. Joshua and Caroline arrived in the drawing room to find Vincent Singer already there. He had clearly rested and changed from his travelling clothes. Caroline had known him on and off since her marriage, but she still felt uncomfortable in his company. He was very striking to look at: tall and lean with a powerful face, and at present he had a full beard, turning from fair to grey. It was neatly trimmed, although he had allowed his shaggy hair to grow a little long.

8

He turned from the fireplace where he was standing, glanced first at Joshua without speaking to him, then came forward to Caroline.

'Good evening, Mrs Fielding,' he said warmly. He had a rich and exquisitely trained voice, and he never spoke carelessly. 'I hope the journey was not too arduous for you?'

She knew he intended to sound concerned, and yet she felt a tiny stab of self-consciousness, as if he were also reminding her that she was older than the rest of them, and an outsider, unused to the rigours of drama, and the self-discipline that made the players always give of their best. Weariness, hunger, fear and private grief were to be overcome. She admired that in all of them and wanted to equal them; above all so Joshua would never be embarrassed for her.

Now she forced herself to smile at Singer. 'It was a most exhilarating journey,' she lied. 'I have never been to this part of Yorkshire before. I could see, even in the dusk as we approached the town, why Mr Stoker chose to set his story here.'

She had no idea whether he believed her or not, but then she had never been able to read his face. Perhaps instead of trying to read him, and failing, she should make more certain that he could not read her either.

'Do you think so?' he said conversationally. 'I would have preferred Cornwall, myself.'

'Too easily associated with smugglers,' she replied. 'Besides, how would one pass Cornwall by sea from Transylvania, in order to be washed ashore, whatever the storm?'

'You are too literal, ma'am,' he said with a tiny shake of his head. 'The whole thing is . . . fantastical.'

'Not at all,' she insisted. 'It is created out of the darkness of the nightmares within us. It must be consistent in itself or it loses its edge of horror.' Her mind flickered back to the past, and the terror that had surrounded and devastated her own family, sixteen years ago. She forced it away again and turned to face Alice Netheridge, who came forward from where she had been standing by the curtains. She was not pretty in the usual way, but there was great emotion in her face, and when she smiled – as she did now – there was a way in which she was quite beautiful.

'Mrs Fielding.' She held out her hand. 'You are marvellously perceptive. That is exactly what I feel too. Dracula is the demon within us. I wish I could put it more successfully on paper. I'm Alice Netheridge.' She turned to Joshua, some little distance behind Caroline, and now she was clearly nervous. She had tried desperately hard to force her ideas into form and she was waiting for his judgement. She might aspire to be an actress adequate for the very small parts she would have to fulfil in the play, but she had no skill to conceal the vulnerability in her eyes now.

Joshua took her hand briefly and smiled at her. 'We will see how it reads tomorrow,' he replied. 'There are always changes; please don't feel badly if we make a few. The spoken word is very different from the written one. If we are any good at our parts, we may need to say far less than you imagine.' He turned to Singer. 'Good evening, Vincent. How was your journey?'

'Tedious,' Singer replied. 'But mercifully uneventful. The weather is vile, and apparently likely to get worse.'

'Then it is fortunate that the house is so comfortable and we shan't have to leave it,' Joshua retorted.

The door opened and they were joined by Lydia Rye, the actress who would play the second female lead, Lucy Westenra, Dracula's first victim. She was pretty in a delicately voluptuous way, and yet there was character in her face and her slightly husky voice was unusually attractive. Caroline had often wondered why she had not overtaken Mercy Carstairs in the leading roles.

'Too little hunger,' Joshua had said, but looking at her now Caroline could not understand what he meant. It was just another example of the way in which she was never quite one of them. She could learn all she wished but she did not have the instinctive understanding the others shared.

Lydia was introduced to Alice, and then to Mr and Mrs Netheridge. Lydia spoke to Joshua and Caroline with the warmth she had always shown, and they were talking agreeably of nothing in particular when the last two of the players arrived. Mercy Carstairs and James Hobbs had been married for three years and seemed well suited to each other. She was very slender, wide-eyed and filled with a restless energy, which on the stage commanded attention. He was traditionally handsome, as tall as Vincent Singer but far less dynamic. He was good in romantic leads but he had no inner darkness at his command to play villains, and no silence within from which to summon tragedy.

They all exchanged greetings, expressed their satisfaction at the ample accommodation that had been given them, then swapped a few stories of the journey from London.

They had already been shown into the dining room and taken their places at the table when the last of the company arrived. He was introduced as Douglas Paterson, fiancé of Alice Netheridge. He was in his late twenties, with a keen face. At the moment he was clearly unable to hide his discomfort at the present gathering. He took his seat with a brief apology, directed first to Mrs Netheridge, then to Alice.

Alice accepted it without comment.

Caroline glanced at Joshua, and saw that he too had recognised the first sign of disapproval. Paterson's glance at Alice, and then the strange tension in his face at her lack of response, made the situation clear. He did not wish his fiancée to be wasting her time in such inappropriate pursuits. He had probably expressed his displeasure earlier, and Alice had chosen to ignore him. If she had misunderstood before, she could not possibly do so now.

The meal was generous and very well served. They began with soup, then fresh fish. Netheridge remarked that it had come in overnight and been brought up from the docks that morning.

'I doubt we'll get more for a while,' he said, looking at the closed curtains beyond which the sound of the rising wind was quite clear.

'They'll put it in ice,' Eliza assured him. 'We have plenty to last us.' She looked at her guests one by one. 'I always find a stormy Christmas quite enjoyable, especially if there is snow. I can remember some years when Christmas Day was so beautiful it was as if the whole world had been made anew while we slept.'

'So it had,' Caroline responded quickly. 'At least in a spiritual sense, and that is how we should see everything.'

Singer stared at her in amazement. 'I thought you were Jewish,' he said, pointedly looking at Joshua and then back at her, his eyebrows high.

There was total silence around the table. Alice dropped her fork and it clattered onto her plate.

Caroline hesitated. She knew everyone was looking at her, waiting to see how she would react. All the players were aware of Joshua's race, but had the Netheridges been, or not? She was so angry she put down her own knife and fork and hid her hands in her lap because they were shaking.

She forced herself to smile charmingly at Vincent. 'No you didn't. You know perfectly well that Joshua is Jewish and I am Christian. You made the remark to be absolutely certain that our host and hostess are also aware of it, although I can't think why, unless it is a desire to embarrass someone. If they now wish us to leave, then you have sabotaged the whole project, and all that hangs on it. Surely that was not your intention?'

For several pulsing seconds the silence returned. The colour washed up Vincent's face as he fought for an answer.

13

Beside Caroline, Joshua shifted uncomfortably. Lydia stared at the floor; Mercy and James looked at each other.

It was Alice who finally spoke, turning to face Joshua.

'It would be terrible if you were to leave, Mr Fielding. You are most welcome here. In fact we cannot possibly succeed without you – either with the play, or with being the kind of hosts we wish to be. How could we celebrate Christmas if we were to turn anyone away into the snow, let alone our own guests who have come here specifically to help us?'

Netheridge winced, but so slightly Caroline would not have noticed it had she not been watching him.

Eliza let out her breath in a low sigh.

Douglas Paterson was clearly appalled.

'You'll make an actress yet,' Vincent said drily. 'I look forward to working with you.'

'Liar,' Lydia mouthed the word soundlessly.

'This pork is delicious,' James remarked to no one in particular. 'It must be local.'

'Thank you,' Eliza murmured. She did not correct him that it was mutton.

After the meal, finished with stilted conversation and very occasional nervous laughter, Caroline found herself being shown over the rest of the very large house by Alice Netheridge and Douglas Paterson. It began very formally, as a matter of courtesy. None of them was particularly interested, but it was an easy thing to do, and filled the time until it would be acceptable to excuse themselves and retire to bed.

Alice was clearly eager to make up for the earlier discomfort, although it had had nothing to do with her.

'Do let me show you the stage,' she said eagerly. 'It was originally designed for music: trios and quartets and that sort of thing. One of my aunts played the cello, or the viola, I can't remember. Grandmama said she was very talented, but of course it's not the sort of thing a lady does, except for the entertainment of her own family.' She glanced at Caroline as she said it, her soft face pulled into an expression of impatience.

'She was thinking of her daughter's welfare,' Douglas pointed out from a step behind her as they walked along the broad corridor. The walls were hung with paintings of Yorkshire coastal scenery. Some were very dark but, looking at them, Caroline thought it was more probable that time had dulled the varnish on them rather than that the artists' intentions had been that they be so forbidding.

'She was thinking of the family's reputation for being proper,' Alice corrected him. 'It was all about what the neighbours would think.'

'You can't live in society without neighbours, Alice,' he replied. He sounded patient, but Caroline saw the flicker of irritation in his face – at least that was what she thought it was. 'You have to make some accommodation to their feelings.'

'I will not have my life ruled by my neighbours' prejudices,' Alice retorted. 'Poor Aunt Delia did, and never played her viola, or whatever it was, except in the theatre here.'

Without realising it, she increased her pace. Caroline was obliged to stride out to keep up with her.

'I imagine she still gave a great deal of pleasure.' Caroline tried to imagine the frustration of that young woman she had never known, and wondered if Alice had known her, or was simply putting herself in her aunt's place.

Alice did not reply.

'She married very happily and had several children,' Douglas put in, catching up with Caroline and walking beside her. 'There is no need whatever to feel sorry for her. She was an excellent woman.'

Alice stopped abruptly and turned to face him. He very nearly walked into her before seeing what she had done.

Caroline thought of her own second daughter, Charlotte, who had been wilful, full of spirit and fire like Alice, and impossible to deter from following her own path, however awkward. She had married socially far beneath herself, at the time, but since then her husband had risen spectacularly. Charlotte had always been happy, in her own way, perhaps the happiest of all her daughters.

Caroline looked at Alice Netheridge facing her fiancé, head high, eyes blazing, and felt a protective warmth towards her. It was as if she had for an instant seen her own daughter as a young woman again, struggling to defy the rules, and follow her own dream. She longed to be able to help Alice, but knew that to interfere would be disastrous. She did not know the girl. All kinds of arrogant mistakes could spring from such a well-meaning thought.

16

'Excellent?' Alice challenged. 'What does that mean? That she did her duty, as her husband saw it?'

Douglas kept his temper with an effort even Caroline, who did not know him, could see. To Alice it must have been as clear as daylight.

'As she saw it herself, Alice,' he said. 'I met her, if you remember? She was gracious, composed, a good wife and a loving mother. You should not forget that. Playing the viola, like any other pastime, is a fine thing to do, in its place. Aunt Delia knew what that place was, and she still played occasionally at supper parties and was much admired.'

'For what? Playing well, or having given up being brilliant in order to be dutiful?' Alice challenged him.

'Living a life of love and generosity mixed with duty, rather than chasing after self-indulgence and an illusion of fame,' he told her. 'Only in the end to be old, lonely and probably destitute among strangers.'

'Lie to yourself that you are happy when all you mean is that you are safe,' she interpreted. 'If you take risks then of course they may turn out badly. But if you marry, that can turn out badly too.' She glanced at him, her lips closed tightly as if to stop them betraying her by trembling. 'And so can having children. Not all children grow up to be charming and obedient. They can be anything: wanton, spiteful, spendthrift, drink too much, even steal. Nothing is certain in life, except that you should not be too afraid of it to accept its challenges.'

'You are very young, Alice.' He still kept his voice under

weary control, but Caroline could see the edge of fear in him now. He did not understand her, and mastery of the situation was slipping out of his grasp. She felt a twinge of pity for him, even though it was Alice she understood so much better.

'I am working on getting older!' Alice snapped, and swung round again to continue on towards the theatre.

Douglas reached out to grasp her arm, but Caroline prevented him. She stepped a yard or so in front of the path he would have to take, making it impossible.

'Don't,' she said quietly enough that Alice would not hear her. Her own footsteps, and the rustle of her skirts drowned it out. 'We probably none of us know whether Aunt Delia was happy or not. The point is that Alice imagines herself in Delia's place, and feels trapped for her. You see her as gracefully letting go of an unreality and embracing a better path.'

He looked at her with surprise. 'Of course I do. Wouldn't anyone, if they thought about it without theatre footlights in their eyes?'

Caroline smiled at him; it was almost a laugh. 'Perhaps. But then I can't say. I have the same lights in my eyes. Or had you not noticed?'

'Oh.' He blinked. For a moment he looked far younger, and not at all unattractive. 'I'm so sorry . . . I . . .'

'Think nothing of it,' she said cheerfully. 'Let us allow Alice to show us the stage, and all its charms and limitations. She will do it anyway. We may as well be gracious about it.'

18

He did not move. 'Do you think this . . . play . . . will come to anything?' There was a real anxiety in his eyes. 'Is she . . . talented?'

Caroline read a world of fear behind the words. Was Alice bored with Whitby, even with Douglas himself? To him the theatre was a tawdry world of make-believe, while to her it was the wings of imagination, the gateway to freedom of the mind, an inner life far brighter than any outer clay could be.

'I don't know,' she admitted, remembering that Joshua had said the play was desperately amateur, close to unwork-able. 'But if she has the courage to put it to the test, you will win nothing at all by preventing her from finding out.'

The flicker crossed his face again. 'She may be hurt. It's my place to try and save her from that.'

'You can't,' Caroline said simply. 'All you can do is comfort her if she fails. You will learn that when you have children. Nothing in the world hurts quite like seeing your child fail, and trying to face the pain of it. But you must not make them fail by preventing them from trying. That really is telling them that you don't believe in either their ability or their courage. Believe me, Mr Paterson, I have daughters just as wilful as Alice, if not more so.'

He looked startled. 'Did they want to write plays?'

'No, but one of them wanted to marry a policeman, and live on a pittance.'

He swallowed. 'What did you do?'

'I let her. Not that I imagine I could have stopped her,' she

19

admitted. 'It was a matter of doing it graciously, or ungraciously. I am delighted to say that she is very happy indeed.'

He was clearly not sure whether to believe her or not.

'Let us join Alice, and be shown the theatre.' She took his arm, so he was obliged to leave the subject and do as she commanded.

After seeing the stage, which was unexpectedly impressive, Caroline returned along the series of corridors to the main part of the house. She found that Joshua had apparently gone to discuss the following day's arrangements with the rest of the players. Only Mr and Mrs Netheridge were in the large withdrawing room. Caroline had barely had time to notice the décor before. They had actually approached the dining room from the far side, and seen this room only through the double doors.

Inside it was awe-inspiring; certainly the key room in the house. The ceiling was unusually high and ornate. She tried to imagine how long the scrolled and curlicued plasterwork must have taken to put in place, and gave up before her staring became too obvious to be good-mannered. The walls were separated into panels, but the most remarkable feature was a window of almost cathedral-like proportions and delicate leaded glass, most of it in rich autumnal colours. It was clearly visible because the curtains were drawn back and held by thick silk ropes. Lanterns on the outside shone through the coloured glass.

Mr Netheridge saw her looking.

'My father had that built,' he said proudly. 'Talk of the town, it was, back then. And folk take it for granted now – least from the outside they do.'

'I can imagine it,' Caroline said truthfully. Whether you cared for it or not, it was certainly impossible to ignore.

Netheridge was pleased. 'Whole room designed around it, of course,' he went on. 'My mother did it all. Had a wonderful eye, didn't she, Eliza?'

'Wonderful,' Eliza agreed drily. Caroline caught the look of sudden loss in her face, but Mr Netheridge was turned the other way. His gaze was wandering yet again over the richly coloured walls – too richly for Caroline's taste. She found the shading oppressive and longed for something cooler, less absorbing of the light. She wondered if Mrs Netheridge senior had been as dominating as her ideas of design were, and if Eliza, as a new bride, had felt obliged to subordinate her own tastes.

Caroline looked at her again and saw a momentary unhappiness in her that was so sharp as to make her feel as if she had unintentionally intruded. She wanted to make amends for it immediately, as if it had not really happened.

'It is quite unlike anywhere I have been before,' she said with forced cheerfulness. Perhaps she would make as good an actress as Lydia or Mercy, one day. 'And it is so extraordinarily comfortable. For all its richness, it still feels like someone's home.' That was a total lie, enough to make her teeth ache, but she saw the pride in Netheridge's face, and the relief in Eliza's.

'We're glad you came,' Netheridge said with satisfaction. 'It'll give our Alice a real chance. Bit of fun for her, before she settles down to married life.'

Eliza said nothing.

Caroline slept well because she was too tired to move. Even when she heard Joshua's voice speaking her name, and felt his hand on her shoulder, she had to battle to the surface of consciousness. She opened her eyes to sharp, white winter daylight and it took a moment or two to remember where she was.

Joshua was smiling. 'Sorry,' he said gently. 'Have I landed you with a wretched Christmas?'

'Probably,' she replied. 'But listening to Eliza Netheridge in that awful drawing room yesterday evening, I thought of my mother-in-law, Edward's mother, and blessed your name for having rescued me from her.'

'Oh, Grandmama.' He rolled his eyes. 'That was my impersonation of St George, rescuing the maiden from the dragon. Was she pretty awful, old Mrs Netheridge? I believe she died over ten years ago.'

'She won't lie down,' Caroline said, sitting up in bed and pushing her long hair out of the way. It was soft and shining, and still mostly dark brown. She rinsed it in a solution of cold tea and iron filings, but she would rather that Joshua did not know that. 'She designed the décor, and it has remained untouched since then,' she went on.

'It must have been redecorated in ten years!' he protested.

'Certainly, but not changed.' She looked at him. 'It's awful, isn't it?'

'Ghastly.' He leaned forward and kissed her softly, intimately, then stood up. 'After breakfast I have to read through this play. I don't know what on earth I'm going to do to make it work. It's bad on the page, and I've an awful fear it's going to be even worse when it's read.'

'We have a few days to work on it.' She pushed the bedclothes away and swung her feet out. 'Let's at least enjoy breakfast. I shall probably eat far too much while I'm here. Judging from dinner last night, they have an excellent cook, and nothing in the kitchen is my responsibility. That in itself makes it all taste better.'

The meal lived up to every expectation. The sideboard groaned under the weight of chafing dishes of kidneys, bacon, sausages, potatoes, and eggs: boiled, scrambled, poached and fried. There was porridge for those who wished it, and racks of toast with butter, jam and marmalade, and pots of tea. It was only the temper of the guests that was sour.

Vincent Singer barely spoke, but that was usual for him in the mornings. Lydia Rye was cheerful, which irritated Mercy.

'I don't know why we are bothering,' she said for the third time. 'Look at the weather. Nobody's going to be able to come for the performance, even if they wish to.' She reached for the marmalade.

'Why wouldn't they wish to?' Lydia asked with exaggerated innocence. '*Dracula* is all the rage in London. Everyone is reading it, simply not to be left out. It will be enormous

23

fun. Don't you want to be Mina, and fall into the arms of the vampire, become one of the "children of the night"?' She sipped her tea delicately.

Mercy glared at her. 'All I can say is thank God you die near the beginning!'

'But then I am "undead"!' Lydia said with a grin. 'It isn't until much later that I can go into the audience and watch all the rest of you without having to worry about remembering any more lines.'

'That's if we can make it workable in the first place,' James said darkly. He had taken a liberal breakfast and was still eating it: kidneys, bacon, egg and sausage.

'We must,' Joshua reminded them. 'A good deal of our survival in the early part of next year depends on it. And I suggest that next time you find a line difficult or an entry or an exit clumsy, you remember that, and try a bit harder.'

Alice Netheridge appeared. The conversation instantly became polite and trivial.

Half an hour later they were assembled in the theatre with copies of the script, ready to begin. Joshua was on the stage both to direct and to play the part of Dracula.

Caroline watched as they began a trifle awkwardly. In the original story, there had been several more characters. Principal among them were Dr Seward, the physician in a lunatic asylum, and Renfield, Seward's patient, the unfortunate man who became the creature of Dracula, obsessed with eating flies and small rodents, in the belief that their

24

life force was necessary to his own survival. Alice had adapted the story so that Seward could be done without, and Renfield only referred to.

Joshua understood and approved the reduction in numbers, for practical reasons of cast. Also, in a single hour, an unfamiliar audience would find too many people confusing to identify. They were left with only Van Helsing; the hero, Jonathan Harker, who was in love with Mina and yet helpless to save her; Mina; Lucy, who was Dracula's first victim; and of course Dracula himself.

Even Caroline, who now knew the story rather better than she had any real wish to, found the reading difficult to follow.

Harker's part had been enlarged so that he recounted the unfortunate Renfield's visit to Dracula's castle in Transylvania and his falling victim to the vampire. He mentioned only briefly Harker's return to England and Renfield's subsequent incarceration in Seward's asylum.

Alice had kept Whitby as the setting, for the most obvious of reasons.

For the first reading there was no movement, although they were all reasonably familiar with their lines. As it had been adapted, Harker was telling Mina, his fiancée, about Renfield's travels to Transylvania, and his present tragic condition. She was listening, appalled and sympathetic.

Caroline had not watched many rehearsals before. Were they always so wooden? James was reading Harker as if he were half asleep. Was he saving his emotion for later, when there were actions to go with the words?

She turned to Alice, sitting beside her, and saw the tension in her face, the tightness where she was biting her lip. Did the words sound stilted to her also? Was she embarrassed by them now?

On the stage, Mercy, as Mina, responded. Her voice rose and fell with emotion that sounded totally artificial, ridiculous when coupled with the banal words she was saying.

Caroline began to feel more and more uncomfortable. She found herself fidgeting in her seat, unable to relax. She knew Joshua well enough to see the frustration in the way he moved and hear it in his voice when he told James to read the lines again.

Mercy came to her husband's defence instantly.

'There's no point yet,' she said sharply. 'We'll only change it. We'll have to. Nobody speaks like this.'

A flicker of anger crossed Joshua's face. Caroline could see the difficulty with which he controlled it.

'Most dialogue sounds inappropriate if you read it like a railway timetable,' he replied. 'You're describing how a normal, decent man has become changed into an insane, disgusting creature. We are supposed to be giving the audience some taste of the horror to come.'

'All so we can be appalled when you appear,' Vincent said drily. 'Rather an old trick, don't you think?'

'Well, there's not much point in Van Helsing's battle against Dracula if he isn't appalling, is there?' Joshua shot back. 'I won't ask you if you want to direct, because I know perfectly well that you do. But right now it's my responsibility, so concentrate on your own job.'

Vincent shrugged elaborately and sighed.

'Move on to the next scene,' Joshua instructed, his voice strained.

It was no better. It was the first appearance of Dracula, having come ashore in a violent storm, which had wrecked his ship and washed up his coffin on the shore. There was no possible way of showing this on the stage, so it had to be represented by one of the actors and had been built into Lydia's part as Lucy Westenra. She too sounded as if she barely believed what she was saying, but there was no sharp edge to her voice, no anger as there was to Mercy's.

'For heaven's sake, Lucy, act it!' Mercy said furiously. 'How do we know if it works or not if you don't try?'

Lucy read it again, with more emotion, and even Caroline had to admit it sounded better. She glanced at Alice Netheridge and saw some of the embarrassment slip away from her expression.

The addition of Dracula's presence improved the drama considerably. The next couple of scenes were quite good. Van Helsing made his appearance.

'I don't think that's strong enough,' Vincent commented. 'He sounds as if he doesn't know what he's doing.'

'He doesn't, yet,' Joshua argued.

'Yes, he does,' Vincent answered immediately. 'He's a genius and he's made a life study of vampires. He has to be powerful. After all, he destroys Dracula, the greatest vampire of all.' He sat back a little in his chair, smiling.

'That's at the end,' Joshua said with markedly less patience. 'If we know that at the beginning then there is no story.'

'Everybody knows the end anyway,' Vincent argued. 'Most people have either read the damn book or they've heard people talking about it.'

Lydia rolled her eyes. 'Vincent, you're an actor. Pretend you don't know, for heaven's sake, or we'll be here all day and go nowhere.'

Vincent turned to her. 'And where exactly is it that you think we are going, my dear?' he asked sarcastically.

'I have no idea,' Lydia replied. 'Any more than you have.'

'Quietly mad!' Mercy put in very distinctly.

'Not a long journey,' Caroline muttered. She was embarrassed when she realised Alice had heard her, until she saw the sudden smile on Alice's face.

'You said "quietly",' Joshua looked at Mercy. 'Make that a promise, will you!'

She glared at him.

'Page thirty-nine, from the top,' Joshua resumed. 'Van Helsing to Harker.'

'We really need another character here,' Vincent pointed out. 'It doesn't make sense like this. Harker's an idiot, completely ineffectual. Van Helsing would neither turn to him nor try to use him.'

'He'll use what he has,' Joshua snapped. 'And at the moment

he has no one else. Just read it, we'll make what amendments we need to later.'

With elaborate patience Vincent did as he was told. It sounded ridiculous, as he had intended it to.

They stopped at lunchtime, having read through the whole hour-long script about twice. The meal was awkward, everyone concentrating on their food, which again was plentiful and afforded an excellent choice. They spoke of trivial things: places they had travelled to at one time or another; books they had read; even the weather – although that last subject had become less trivial as the wind increased and the snow, which had been falling intermittently, became heavier. It was clear from the almost horizontal angle it was streaming past the windows, and the thrashing of the trees beyond, that it was increasing in violence.

'I think of those at sea,' Eliza said unhappily, staring at the snow-blinded glass. 'I feel almost guilty to be so safe.'

'I can't imagine why anyone wants to go to sea, especially in the winter,' James observed.

'They probably don't,' Vincent looked at him witheringly. 'Poor devils have little choice. We can't all be actors.'

'Indeed we can't,' Joshua retorted. 'Not even all those of us who try.'

Lydia laughed, then winced as apparently someone kicked her under the table.

Douglas Paterson looked at her with quick appreciation,

then straightened his face again and pretended he was not amused.

After the meal, Joshua asked if he might speak with Netheridge, and ten minutes later was in Netheridge's study. It was a large, extremely comfortable room with leather-covered armchairs. A huge oak desk was littered with the implements of writing: pens, paper, two inkwells, a sand tray, sticks of sealing wax in various shades of red, matches and tapers, and several penknives and paper knives. The walls were lined with books, set by subject rather than size, as if they were there for use. A fire burned briskly in the hearth.

Joshua had asked Caroline to accompany him.

'I can't help,' she had said, meaning it as an apology, not an excuse.

'Yes you can,' he had told her with a tiny, twisted smile. 'If you are there at least he will hesitate to lose his temper. So will I.'

Unfortunately, Douglas Paterson was present also. Since he was Alice's fiancé it was difficult to claim that he had no interest.

Netheridge stood in front of the fire. Joshua accepted the invitation to be seated, even though it placed him at something of a disadvantage. Caroline sat opposite him, already feeling defensive, in spite of the agreeable smiles on everyone's faces. Douglas Paterson stood over by the window, his back to the ever-increasing storm.

'Well, Mr Fielding, how is it going?' Netheridge asked.

'Do you have everything you require? Is there anything else we can provide for you?'

Caroline felt her throat tighten.

'We have read through the script a couple of times, to see how it works,' Joshua replied. 'That is customary for a new piece. What seems powerful on the page does not always translate to natural speech.'

Netheridge grinned but he did not interrupt.

It was Paterson who spoke. 'Is this the beginning of an excuse to say you cannot perform it?'

Joshua swung round in his chair to face him. 'No, Mr Paterson. If that were what I meant to say I would be plainer about it. Mr Netheridge deserves the truth, as far as we can discern it.'

'The truth is that Alice has some rather impractical dreams, and it would be better if you didn't indulge her in them.' Paterson was blunt.

Caroline remembered Alice's face as she sat in the audience chairs and listened to her words read on the stage: the awe, the excitement and hope, the embarrassment. Joshua must make it work, although she had no idea how.

'I won't insult you by suggesting that that is other than the truth as you see it,' Joshua answered Paterson. 'As I see it, it is a work that needs some attention. Possibly the order of certain scenes should be changed, so that we can give it the passion and drive it requires to move it from one medium to another.'

'Are you saying you can do it?' Netheridge challenged.

Joshua hesitated only a second, but Netheridge saw it. His jaw hardened. 'You doubt it!' he challenged him. 'Be honest, man. Alice is my only child. She's wilful, a dreamer, perhaps a little naïve, but I'll not have her made a fool of, by you or anyone else.'

Paterson smiled, and his tight shoulders eased a little. The shadow of a smile softened his face.

Netheridge looked at Joshua. 'Are you prepared to work at this thing and make it right? Give me a straight answer, man.'

Joshua took a deep breath, then let it out slowly. The clock on the mantelpiece over the fire moved two seconds. 'Yes, I am.'

'Right! Then what is it you want of me, Mr Fielding? The party is set for Boxing Day. Can't change that now,' Netheridge said with a frown.

'I understand,' Joshua replied. 'We will have to work very hard. I will need the time without interruption other than for meals. Possibly I might request to eat in the theatre room, if the cook would be kind enough to allow me something simple that can be served there. And perhaps Mrs Netheridge would help my wife to find a few articles we might borrow as props to dress the stage?'

'Done,' Netheridge said. 'She'll be delighted. What else?'

'A good supply of paper and ink, more than I thought to bring with me. But most of all I would appreciate your assistance and even support in explaining to Miss Netheridge that this is necessary if we are to make the play a success—'

'A success?' Paterson interrupted. 'We're doing this as a Christmas gift for Alice, not to perform on the London stage. How on earth do you judge what is a success? If it pleases her, that's all that matters. If it isn't going to work, then perhaps the most honest thing would be to tell her so now, and save her being humiliated in front of her friends, and her family's friends, the people she will mix with long after you have all gone back to London, or wherever it is you come from.' There were two spots of pink on his cheeks and he had moved a step closer towards them.

'A success will be something that entertains and enthrals an audience, Mr Paterson,' Joshua replied, his voice gathering emotion. 'Something that suspends their disbelief for an hour, makes them laugh or cry, think more deeply or create new dreams in their minds. And a failure is something that bores them, has no integrity within itself, and does not even for a moment take them somewhere they have not been before. If we are to capture and hold their imagination then we must iron out the inconsistencies and improve on the strengths.'

'Then why are you here instead of in the theatre doing that?' Paterson asked, but his tone had lost its belligerence. He looked puzzled and anxious.

Caroline realised how far out of his depth he was. He did not know Alice as well as he had imagined he did, and understanding this frightened him.

'Because Alice needs your support,' she answered for Joshua. 'When you have created something there is so much of yourself in it that it is very hard to accept criticism. We

33

all need praise as well as showing where things could be better. We need those we love to believe that we can succeed.'

Douglas chewed his lip, glanced at Netheridge, then back, not at Caroline, but at Joshua. 'If you change it into your work, what will be left of it that is hers?' There was uncertainty in his eyes, and still a degree of challenge.

Netheridge nodded. 'Yes, Mr Fielding. Douglas is right. If you change it as much as you say, whatever our friends think, she'll know it isn't hers. And she's honest, Alice is. She won't take the credit for your work.'

Caroline looked at him still standing in front of the fire: the son of a self-made man who had increased his father's fortune and who now owned more than all his ancestors put together, a man who loved his only child but did not believe in her talent. And perhaps he was right not to. Joshua had said the play, as it stood, was unperformable. What answer could Joshua give that would be even remotely honest?

'I'm not going to rewrite it for her,' Joshua said softly. 'I'm going to help her rewrite it herself. It will still be hers, but with a lot more knowledge of what stagecraft can do.'

'Ah.' Netheridge looked pleased. 'Good,' he said firmly. He turned to look at Paterson. 'Told you, Douglas, got a good man here. Right you are, Mr Fielding. You'll get everything you need from me. Thank you for your honesty.'

Joshua rose to his feet and straightened his shoulders. Perhaps only Caroline, who knew him so well, could see the overwhelming relief in him.

When they were outside the door and it was closed again behind them, he turned to her with a shaky smile.

'Thank you,' he said in a whisper.

She found herself suddenly absurdly emotional. Her own voice was husky when she spoke. 'How are you going to do it?'

'I have no idea,' he admitted. 'God help me, it's probably beyond anyone else's ability.'

She moved a little closer to him and slipped her hand into his. She felt his fingers tighten, warm and strong. She wanted to say something encouraging, full of certainty, but it would have been a lie. He would have known it too, so she said nothing, just held onto him.

Caroline found Eliza delighted to help.

'I'm sure we can find all sorts of things,' she said eagerly when Caroline asked her. 'Just tell me what you need.'

Caroline had already given it much thought. It was of great importance to her that she help Joshua, because their success mattered so much to the company, but also she had a hunger to be part of the production, not merely an onlooker. Too often she had been in the company simply because she was Joshua's wife, present only on the edge of emotion and the companionship.

'We need something to suggest Mina's home,' she replied, and Eliza led the way to one of the boxrooms where unused furniture was stored. 'Chairs, perhaps? And a spare curtain, if you have one. It would suggest warmth, and height. I think

35

that would be good. We can't have anything too heavy to move.'

'Oh, yes, I see.' Eliza opened the door to the boxroom and led the way in. It was piled with all kinds of discarded chairs, tables, cupboards, cushions and curtains, a couple of cabin trunks, two or three carved boxes. There were also a lot of jardinières, lamp brackets and some large, colourful vases that would not have fitted anywhere in the parts of the house Caroline had seen.

Eliza saw her glance and gave a tiny, rueful smile. 'Choices I shouldn't have made,' she said quietly.

'I like them,' Caroline responded before she thought. The colours were warm and unusual.

'So do I,' Eliza agreed, biting her lip. 'But they don't fit in with my mother-in-law's taste.' She did not offer any further explanation, but it was unnecessary. The stamp of a dominant personality was heavy in every room Caroline had seen so far.

'My mother-in-law's taste would have been good for a funeral parlour,' she said sympathetically. 'One would quite naturally have felt in mourning, whether you had lost anyone or not.'

Eliza gave a little giggle, and then stifled it quickly, as if she should not have been amused. She met Caroline's eyes in a glance full of humour. 'Just right for a vampire story, don't you think?' she asked, then blushed.

Caroline found herself liking her immensely. 'Perfect. But thank goodness she's safely in London with my younger daughter. If we could use that red vase with the flowers it would give Mina's house something warm and bright, and people would remember it and know immediately where they are again.' She looked around the room. 'We could use that dark curtain over there to suggest the crypt where Lucy is buried.'

Eliza gasped, then burst into laughter, her hands flying to her mouth to stifle it.

'I'm sorry, is that not . . . acceptable?' Caroline felt awkward.

'No, no, it's perfect!' Eliza shook her head, dismissing the apology. 'It was Mother-in-law's favourite. It took some five years to get it out of the withdrawing room. Charles and I still have disagreements over it.' The laughter vanished.

'Would you rather not remind him of it?' Caroline offered. 'Or maybe it would hurt his feelings, do you think? I mean if we use it to suggest . . . a crypt?'

'It's perfect for a crypt,' Eliza said decisively. 'It looks like grave hangings anyway. Let's see what else we can find.'

Caroline took a deep breath and followed after Eliza among the piles of furniture. She hoped she was not going to cause this warm and vulnerable woman more heartache after they were gone.

Joshua spent the afternoon attempting to rewrite at least some of the major outline of the play. It was a difficult work for an amateur to adopt, particularly because, like many novels, much of the tension came from the characters' inner thoughts, and were impossible to dramatise without creating scenes that did not exist in the original.

There were also a great many letters, impossible to translate into action.

Alice had done a good job of cutting the story to exclude these, and still make sense, but there were awkward transitions, which still needed quite a lot of work.

The weather became worse, the wind rising so that the snow drifted, piling up against banks and leaving the lee side almost bare. Trees leaned dangerously, cracking under the weight of the snow. Some lighter branches broke.

Joshua barely noticed, but Caroline, staring out of the windows at a leaden sky late in the afternoon, realised that there was a great likelihood of their being snowed in, perhaps for several days. They had intended to be there until well after Christmas, but she still found it a curiously imprisoning thought.

It was late afternoon and already dark. She was crossing the hallway when the doorbell rang. It was so startling, considering the weather, that she stopped where she was at the bottom of the stairs as the footman appeared and went to answer it. He pulled the door wide open, peering forward a little as if he expected to see no one on the step.

He was mistaken, and Caroline heard his gasp from twenty feet away. She too stared at the man who stood silhouetted against the snow-whirled darkness. He was of at least average height, his hair was smooth and black, and the shoulders of his cloak were covered in pale, glistening

38

snow. The lamplight from inside made his cheeks hollow, his eyes under the dark brows so black as to seem without pupils.

'Good evening,' he said softly, but his voice carried with startling clarity, his diction perfect. 'I apologise for disturbing you on such a night, but circumstances have forced me to seek your help. My name is Anton Ballin, and my carriage has broken down in a drift some way from here. I have left my coachman at the wheelwright's, but I must ask for shelter for myself.'

The footman had no civilised alternative but to ask the man in.

'Please step inside, Mr Ballin. Give me your cloak, sir, and warm yourself by the fire. I shall inform my master of your situation.'

'You are most kind.' Ballin came inside, as requested. As he crossed the light it was possible to see that he was carrying a small case, such as one might have for a single night's stay somewhere. He looked at Caroline.

'Madame,' he inclined his head. He was striking in appearance. He would have been handsome were his cheekbones not a little too prominent and his skin unnaturally pale. 'I regret imposing on your hospitality,' he added with a very slight shrug. 'The weather is far worse than I had anticipated.'

Caroline realised that he spoke with a very faint accent. It was more a precision of diction than any alteration of vowels.

She came forward. 'I am Caroline Fielding, another guest,

39

but I am sure Mrs Netheridge will make you welcome for as long as this weather lasts.' She offered her hand.

He took it gently. His hands were gloved, and freezing. He raised hers to his lips in the gesture of a kiss, then let it fall. He regarded her curiously. Even inside the hall his eyes were as black as they had seemed in the shadows.

'Not another orphan of the storm, I hope?' he asked curiously.

'Not at all, Mr Ballin. My husband and I are here as Mr Netheridge's guests, with a very small company of actors, who are to perform a play for such friends and neighbours as are able to come, on Boxing Day.'

'Fielding,' he rolled the name on his tongue. 'Mr Joshua Fielding?'

Caroline felt a distinct flush of pleasure, even of pride. 'Yes. Do you know him?'

'Of course,' he smiled. He had excellent teeth, even and very white. They gave his face a power she had not appreciated before because it was so dominated by his eyes. 'A fine actor,' he went on. 'He has the ability to convey many moods, many types of people, and carry you with all of them. It is a rare gift. What are you to perform for these fortunate guests of Mr Netheridge's?'

Now she was not so certain that telling him had been a good idea, although if he were to be islanded here by the storm, as seemed inevitable, then he would know soon enough. Still she felt self-conscious in answering.

'An adaptation of Bram Stoker's novel *Dracula*,' she

replied, wishing she could have said it was a few scenes from Shakespeare, or even a reading from Charles Dickens's works.

'Really?' His voice held no incredulity, and certainly no suggestion of disappointment. 'I did not know such a thing had been written. You interest me greatly.'

She felt even more embarrassed, but there was no way of avoiding answering him.

'Miss Netheridge has made an adaptation,' she said with as little hesitation as she could. 'The work is not complete yet, but we are progressing quite well.' That was a massive overstatement. She knew that Joshua's afternoon had been frustrating. He had said he felt even less hopeful than when he had made such rash promises to Charles Netheridge, and by implication to Alice.

She was saved from Ballin's reply by the appearance of Netheridge. He introduced himself to Ballin and made him welcome, offering him hospitality for as long as he should need it. This included a change of clothes from those he was wearing, which were obviously soaked through: small pools of water glistened at his feet in the light from the chandeliers.

Caroline excused herself and went to tell Joshua of Ballin's arrival, and that he knew Joshua and admired him.

Two hours later Ballin joined them at dinner. His clothes had been dried and ironed by Netheridge's valet, and, if he were exhausted by his carriage ordeal or his long walk in the snow, he showed no sign of it at all.

'I hope you were not hurt, Mr Ballin?' Eliza enquired with concern.

'Not at all,' Ballin answered gravely, and yet a certain amusement flickered in his eyes. 'Except my dignity, perhaps. To be riding in comfort, if also in anxiety, at one moment, and then scrambling to arise out of a drift of snow the next, makes one appear more than a little ridiculous. However, there was no one to observe me, except my coachman, and he was in no better circumstances than I.'

'Where is he?' Lydia asked, her soup spoon arrested half-way to her mouth.

'In the servants' quarters, I imagine,' Mercy answered her. 'Did you expect to see him in the dining room?'

Ballin looked at Mercy with interest, his eyes searching her delicate, pretty face as if trying to observe something deeper. 'Actually he is staying at the wheelwright's cottage, Mrs Hobbs,' he answered softly. 'He bruised his legs rather badly and I fear this walk would have been distressing for him.'

'Where were you hoping to go?' James asked. However, there was no interest in his face, merely good manners.

'To stay with friends at the further side of Whitby,' Ballin replied. 'I regret it will be some time before that is possible, to judge from the weather. No doubt they will have deduced that I was obliged to seek hospitality elsewhere, and they will not be overly anxious.'

'Sorry.' Netheridge shook his head. 'Can't get a message to anyone through this. It's several feet deep in some places

42

on the road. And if this wind gets worse, we could have trees down.'

Even as he spoke the howling outside increased. Mercy shivered, glancing towards the rich red curtains drawn across the windows.

'"Listen to the children of the night",' Vincent quoted from *Dracula*, an original line Alice had kept in the play.

Mercy gave another, even more convulsive shiver.

'You're not on stage now!' Lydia said sharply. 'There are no bats or wolves out there. This is Yorkshire.'

'Dracula came to Yorkshire,' Mercy retorted instantly. 'This is exactly where it all happened! Didn't you read it, for heaven's sake?'

'I read it,' Lydia said with a sigh. 'I don't believe it. It's my job to believe it on stage, not at the dinner table.'

'It's only the wind,' James said to no one in particular. 'The whole thing is an excellent horror story, but there's nothing real to be frightened of.'

'Bravo,' Vincent observed sarcastically. 'That's perfectly in character. Harker didn't believe in vampires until Dracula had already taken Lucy and turned her into a vampire herself.'

Alice looked from one to the other of them. Her eyes were bright, and there was a slight flush on her cheeks, although it was impossible to tell if it was embarrassment or excitement, or a little of each.

Douglas Paterson regarded her with distress close to exasperation. 'Really—' he began.

Alice ignored him, looking now at Ballin. 'Can we make you believe in vampires, just for a season?' she asked him.

'Alice!' Netheridge protested.

Ballin held up his long-fingered, powerful hand, moving with unusual grace. 'Please! It is a game we must all play, the suspension of disbelief, just for a while. Surely Christmas is the season in which to believe in miracles? The Son of God came to earth as a little child, helpless and dependent, just as we all are, even when we least think so. Does it not follow that the creatures of evil must also be knocking at the door, waiting for someone to allow them in?'

Mercy gave a little gasp.

Lydia rolled her eyes and turned momentarily to Douglas, and then away again.

Alice was looking at Ballin intently, her expression keen with interest. 'I've never heard anyone say that before,' she said intently.

'Of course you haven't,' Douglas responded. 'It's nonsense.'

'No it isn't!' Caroline said quickly. 'Haven't you seen Holman Hunt's painting of Christ *The Light of the World*? He is standing at the door but the handle is on the inside. If we do not open it ourselves, then he cannot come in either. Maybe the final choice is always ours?'

'What about Hallowe'en?' Mercy asked. 'Aren't demons supposed to be abroad then? Can't they come in?'

'Fairy stories,' Netheridge said briskly. 'Anyway, demons are not the same thing as vampires. The Church might have a reasonable argument for the devil, but vampires

44

are strictly Bram Stoker's imagination. Damned good story, but that's all.'

'If you will forgive me saying so, Mr Netheridge, vampires are a lot older than Mr Stoker, vivid as his imagination is,' Ballin said apologetically. 'And they are not demons,' he turned to Mercy, 'which are essentially inhuman. Vampires are the "undead", who were once as human and mortal as you or I, but who have lost the blessings of death and the resurrection to eternal life. They are damned, in the sense that they can never progress in this way.'

'What the devil are you talking about?' Douglas demanded hotly. 'You are speaking as if they are not the creation of some opportunist writer's desire to make a name and a fortune for himself by trading on the unhealthy fears of a part of society who have time on their hands, and overheated imaginations.'

Netheridge gave him a heavily disapproving look. 'Nonsense,' he said tartly. 'You are making far too much of it, Douglas. A little fear sharpens our appreciation for the very real safety and comfort that we have. Don't spoil the entertainment by sounding so self-righteous.'

Douglas blushed deep red, but said nothing at all.

Eliza looked uncomfortable.

Joshua drew in his breath, and then found he had nothing to say either.

It was Ballin who spoke. 'You give Mr Stoker too much credit, and too much blame, Mr Paterson. His work is very fine. He has created a story that will no doubt entertain readers for decades to come, but he is far from the first to use the ancient figure of the vampire as a literary device. Perhaps it will be even more successful than John Polidori's *The Vampyre*, published nearly eighty years ago. He was a physician, and his vampire, Lord Ruthven, was based upon his illustrious patient, Lord Byron.'

'I think we may very safely presume there is no truth in that,' Joshua put in.

Ballin smiled at him. 'I agree, unequivocally. However, the history of the vampire, real or imagined, goes back even beyond the ancient Greeks, to the Hebrews and the blood-drinking Lilith. The pedigree is perhaps not respectable, but it is certainly rooted in mankind's knowledge of good and evil, and what may become of a human soul when the darkness is chosen over the light.'

Alice was fascinated. The colour in her cheeks had heightened and her eyes were brilliant.

'You know!' she whispered. 'You understand. The evil is real.' She turned to Joshua. 'You are right, Mr Fielding: we haven't caught the essence of the novel yet. I am so grateful to you for not humouring me and letting me go ahead with something so much less than good, let alone true. We must work harder. Perhaps Mr Ballin will help us?'

Lydia looked at Alice, then at Douglas, and her face registered a gamut of emotions. Caroline thought she saw in it more compassion than anything else. Was it for Douglas, or for Alice? Or had she misread it altogether, and it was only fear and a degree of embarrassment?

'If I may be of assistance, without intruding, then I would be honoured,' Ballin replied, first to Alice, then to Joshua.

Caroline watched Joshua, uncertain what she read in his eyes. Was it amusement, desperation, awareness of his own inadequacy to mend a situation that had run away from him like a bolting horse?

'Have you any experience in stagecraft, Mr Ballin?' he asked.

Ballin hesitated for the first time Caroline had seen since he had stepped through the front door out of the storm and into the light and the warmth.

'I think I should leave that to you, Mr Fielding.' He bowed his black head very slightly. 'I should speak only of the legend of the vampire, and what it says of mankind.'

'Legend is just what it is,' Netheridge agreed. 'Like all that Greek nonsense about gods and goddesses always squabbling with each other, and changing shape into animals, and whatever.'

'Ah,' Ballin sighed. 'Metamorphosis. What a wonderful idea: to change completely, at will, into something else. Such an easy dream to understand.'

'Not if it's wolves and bats,' Lydia shuddered. 'Why would anyone want to turn into such a thing?'

'To escape, of course,' Ballin told her. 'It is always to escape. Bats can fly, can steer themselves without sight, moving through the darkness at will.'

Mercy gave a cry, almost a strangled scream.

'Stop playing to the gallery,' Lydia said under her breath,

but Caroline heard her quite clearly. She wondered who else did. James Hobbs looked pale. Joshua was exasperated.

The evening was clearly going to be a very long one.

It did not end as Caroline expected, although looking back on it, perhaps she should have. She was standing at the top of the stairs speaking to Eliza of further pieces for the stage that they might use, when a nerve-jangling scream ripped through the silence, instantly followed by another, and then silence.

A door flew open along the landing and James Hobbs burst out, his hair wild, his shirt half undone. He stared at Caroline and Eliza, then swivelled round to face the opposite direction.

Vincent Singer opened one of the other doors and put his head out. 'What the devil's going on?' he demanded.

'Mercy!' James all but choked.

For a cold instant Caroline thought he had been attacked, then she realised it was not a plea, but his wife's name.

Joshua was coming up the stairs from the hall. He turned on the step and started down again, increasing his pace to a run as he reached the bottom.

Eliza was ashen. 'What is it? What's happened?'

Vincent came out into the landing and closed his bedroom door.

James rushed past Eliza and Caroline and ran down the stairs, all but falling in his haste to take them two at a time, and grasping onto the rail close to the bottom to steady himself.

48

He followed Joshua into the passage that led eventually to the stage.

Caroline started after them, Eliza straight behind her.

There were no more screams, only a thick silence, almost smothering the sound of their footsteps. Caroline could feel her heart beating and she knew she was clumsy, afraid of slipping on the stairs, afraid of being too slow, too late for whatever terrible thing had happened. What were they going to find? Blood? Someone dead? Of course not. That was ridiculous. A maid tripped and fallen, at the worst. Perhaps a broken ankle.

She was hampered by her skirts. Joshua was well ahead of her. She could hear James Hobbs shouting for Mercy.

She bumped into a large Chinese vase filled with ornamental bamboo and set it rocking. She stopped to replace it upright, and Eliza caught up with her.

'Never mind that!' she said breathlessly. 'I always hated it anyway. Come on!' She shoved the whole thing out of her way and it crashed to the floor.

Caroline hesitated, then went after her.

They swung around the last corner before the theatre to find Joshua and James Hobbs facing Mercy. She was leaning against the wall, gasping her breath, her face flushed scarlet.

Opposite her Mr Ballin was standing perfectly composed, some seven or eight feet away from her, his hands at his sides. They all looked at Eliza.

'You have a superb theatre, Mrs Netheridge,' Ballin said frankly. 'Even the sound is flawless. It was designed by someone of the most excellent taste and technical knowledge. I came to look at it, and I regret Mrs Hobbs did not expect to find anyone else here. Quite understandably, I startled her. I am so sorry.'

Joshua swore under his breath with a couple of words Caroline had not heard him use before. She would not have heard them at all had she not been standing close enough almost to touch him.

He steadied himself. 'You have no need to apologise, Mr Ballin. I am sure you intended no harm. Mrs Hobbs's imagination seems to have got the better of her.' He looked at Mercy without trying to conceal his impatience. 'For goodness' sake, Mercy, go to bed and get some sleep. We all need it.'

'Are you sure you are quite all right, Mrs Hobbs?' Eliza said anxiously.

James moved even closer to Mercy, then glared at Ballin. 'Of course she isn't all right! He comes creeping around here, uninvited, and frightens her half to death. Then when she seems in terror, instead of standing back, he follows her. How could she possibly be all right?'

Vincent spread his arms wide. 'Perfect,' he said sarcastically. 'The black-cloaked stranger comes out of the storm, no doubt washed ashore in his coffin, and then stalks young women in the vast heart of this elaborate house with its stained-glass windows and private theatre. I couldn't have designed it better myself. For God's sake, stop being such a damned actress, Mercy. Be a human being for half an hour.'

Lydia, who was standing next to Caroline, started to laugh, and choked it off only with difficulty.

Alice appeared, breathless. 'Is anyone hurt?' she asked anxiously.

'No, of course not,' Vincent snapped. 'Mercy met Mr Ballin round a corner and imagined she met a vampire so she screamed like a banshee, in order that no one in the entire house, and probably half Whitby, would miss her moment of high drama. Go to bed and don't worry about it. It's a rehearsal.' He stalked away and disappeared round the corner back to the main hallway.

Mercy had started to tremble.

Eliza went to her. 'Please let us take you back to the withdrawing room. Perhaps a hot cocoa would warm you. You have had a terrible shock.'

'So must poor Mr Ballin,' Caroline said. 'If he was walking along the corridor quietly and someone came out of the shadows screaming at him at the top of her lungs, she's lucky he didn't have an apoplexy. Mr Ballin, I'm extremely sorry we are all behaving like mad people. We have been rehearsing a play of considerable horror; and we are worried that we will not be able to do the subject justice. We are tired and rather highly strung. I hope you will be quite all right. Perhaps you should have a cup of hot cocoa as well. It will settle your nerves after what must have been a terrible shock for you.'

'If you wander uninvited around other people's houses at night, you must expect to cause terror and distress,' James said angrily.

Joshua clenched his teeth. 'He is not uninvited, James. He offered to help us improve the script and we accepted—'

'*You* accepted!' James snapped back.

'I did, so did Miss Netheridge. It is her play, and I am directing it. Mr Ballin is a guest here.' He turned to Ballin. 'I hope you will sleep well, and still feel like giving us whatever assistance you can in the morning.'

Ballin bowed. 'Of course. Good night.' He walked away slowly, elegantly, perhaps conscious of everyone watching him.

Caroline let out a sigh of relief and leaned closer to Joshua. His arm tightened around her.

In the morning they were all considerably subdued. It was still snowing and, although no one said so, it was apparent that they were effectively imprisoned in the house. The drifts were deep. No vehicle could make its way through them – a man on foot might easily slip and fall, and the snow would bury him. One of the footmen had been as far as the bend of the road, and reported that there were several trees down. They could not reasonably expect to be able to get a dogcart past for a couple of days, even if the weather improved within hours – and it showed no signs of that. The sky was leaden, and every so often there were more squalls of snow.

'Is there any point in rehearsing?' Mercy asked Joshua when she found him walking towards the theatre with Caroline. 'You can't imagine anyone is going to come to an amateur play in this!' She ignored Caroline.

'Weren't you listening to the footman?' Joshua asked her. 'They couldn't even get to a doctor in this. Have you a better idea how we should spend our time until we know whether we are to perform or not?'

'For whom? The kitchen staff?'

'If we can entertain the kitchen staff it would be a good indication that we had made a passable drama out of it,' he retorted. 'But Christmas is still a few days away. A rise in temperature and a day's rain, and the roads will be open again. What else do you want to do?'

'Not play Mina in this damned awful play!'

'And not play on the London stage in the spring either, I presume?'

'All right! I'll do Mina! Get that horrible man to play Dracula and we'll scare the wits out of half the neighbourhood,' she retorted, increasing her stride and moving ahead of him. She barged past Caroline as if she had been curtains on the wall.

The rehearsal began quite well. They started not at the beginning, which still awaited some rewriting, but at a scene where Mina has been attacked once already and Van Helsing discovers the puncture marks of the vampire's teeth in her throat.

Mercy was suitably wan and exhausted. Caroline hated to admit it, even to herself, but she did it rather well. Even James, Douglas Paterson, Lucy and Alice, all sitting in the audience, did not feel inclined to interrupt. Only Joshua seemed weary with it, as if something still did not satisfy him. Caroline did not understand what it was. Once she looked at Mr Ballin, and saw for an instant the same expression in his face.

At the end of the scene they stopped, waiting for instructions as to the next place to work on.

'That was excellent,' James said enthusiastically. 'We are beginning to catch the mood of it.'

'She's still terrified from last night, aren't you!' Lydia challenged them, looking at Mercy with amusement. 'If the real Dracula had met you, you would have died of fright. Not much use to anyone then, even to him.'

Ballin turned towards her.

'I think perhaps you miss the point, Miss Rye, that Dracula is repellent only when one sees his soul. In human form he has great attraction, especially for women.'

'He's evil!' Douglas said sharply. 'We can all see that. That is why he horrifies us. That is the point, surely?'

'No, Mr Paterson,' Ballin spoke gently, caressing the words. 'The very power of evil is that it is not recognisable to us most of the time. It is not repellent at all. It does not attack, it seduces.'

Caroline felt a sudden chill, as if a cold hand had touched her.

Douglas's mouth curled with disgust, and for an instant with something that looked like fear. 'It's a fairy story, Mr Ballin,' he said gratingly. 'An entertainment for Christmas, and I think in very poor taste. But if we must have it, then let us at least be honest about it. The whole idea of vampires is disgusting. If we make that clear then at least we will have done something.'

'We will have lied,' Ballin smiled. 'Do we not all feed upon each other, at times, in some fashion?'

Lydia laughed and gave a brief applause. 'You're wonderful, Mr Ballin. You are giving us exactly the *frisson* of genuine fear we need to make this come alive.' She shot a look at Douglas, her eyes bright and gentle. 'And you play to him perfectly. Did you arrange it?'

Douglas was clearly nonplussed, but he enjoyed the compliment. After a moment's hesitation he decided to make the best of it and smiled slowly, neither confirming nor denying.

Alice was startled. She saw Douglas's gratitude to Lydia, and even a spark of admiration in his face. She was surprised at herself that she felt no jealousy at all.

Watching them all, Caroline too was surprised. Had she been Alice she might have wanted to be the one to charm Douglas, and resented another young and very pretty woman who had done it in her place.

But Alice was thinking of the play. She turned to Ballin. 'I haven't caught that essence of evil yet, have I?' she stated. 'I wanted Dracula to fascinate the audience and make them afraid, but the whole point of the story is that he fascinates Lucy and Mina, in spite of their being good people. It's the potential weakness in all of us that is the really frightening thing.'

'You must invite the vampire into your house or he cannot

enter,' Ballin added. 'That is at the heart of it. Perhaps you might make the point a little more forcefully. You have it, but the audience may miss its importance.'

'Yes. Yes, I will! Mr Fielding was so much more correct than I realised, even yesterday. We have a lot of work to do.'

Douglas looked pained. 'It's only for the neighbours, Alice.'

A shadow of annoyance crossed Alice's face. 'I want to do the best I can for its own sake,' she said a little angrily, as if he should have known her well enough not to need her to say it. 'I'm not upset by it, I'm grateful.'

'You were upset yesterday. You were nearly in tears,' he pointed out.

She stood up, her cheeks flushed with embarrassment that he should have made her humiliation so public. 'Well, I'm not now! You may not care whether I succeed or not, but I care. I want to do the best I can. I want to capture the power and the meaning of it as well as the more superficial horror. I'm sorry you think I'm not worth that, and that I can't do it. But perhaps it's as well I know that of you now.' She walked stiffly past Douglas and Lydia and stopped at the foot of the stage, a couple of yards from where Joshua was standing with the script in his hand.

'I shall come back in a few moments,' she told him. 'I'm not walking out. I just need to think a little.'

Joshua nodded, and watched her leave. Then he looked at Ballin, his face registering both curiosity and respect. Caroline imagined she saw a moment of bright, almost luminous understanding between them.

Douglas looked wretched. Lydia put her hand on his arm, very gently.

'Don't worry so much,' she whispered to him. 'She's nervous because she is trying to do something very difficult, and she wants to do it well. Wouldn't you, especially when you have everybody you care about looking at you? I would.'

He looked at her intensely for several seconds. 'Do you love acting?' he asked impulsively. 'I mean . . . I mean really love it? So you would be wretched if you couldn't do it?'

She lowered her eyes, then looked up at him with a sweet smile. 'No, not at all. It's quite fun, and I like the friendship we have, almost like a family, but I'd still rather have a real family, a husband and children. I think most women would, perhaps not all . . .' She left the idea unfinished, as if it were too indelicate to complete.

He sighed and leaned back in his seat.

Caroline heard Eliza Netheridge breathe in sharply and turned to meet her eyes, feeling as if she knew her thoughts. She had had three daughters herself. Sarah, her eldest, had died some time ago, in circumstances that still touched her with horror. Charlotte, the second and by far the most awkward, had met the man she would eventually marry because of the manner of Sarah's death. Caroline had almost despaired of her, and yet in some ways Charlotte had enriched all their lives through her choice in a way that no one else in the family had. Emily, the youngest, had married brilliantly the first time, then been widowed, and now was happily married again. But Caroline knew exactly what Eliza was suffering. She smiled at her now.

'I wouldn't bother saying anything to her, if I were you,' she said very quietly, so there was no chance of anyone else overhearing her. 'Just now, it would only make it worse. I have a daughter whose nature is not unlike Alice's. She was about as biddable as a domestic cat. I don't know if you have ever tried to make a cat do anything it didn't wish to?'

Eliza smiled in spite of herself. 'Quite pointless,' she replied. 'But I'm still fond of them, and they are both affectionate and very useful in the house.'

'So are wilful daughters, when they are good at heart,' Caroline nodded.

Eliza sighed. 'Alice is good, but she will lose that young man if she is not kinder towards him. I'm sorry if she is a friend of yours, but that young Miss Rye has her eyes on him – I don't know with what intent: to win him, or merely for the fun of playing, like a cat with a mouse, to continue your domestic likeness.'

'From what I know of her, quite possibly to win him.' Caroline surprised herself by the sincerity of her answer. She realised as she spoke how many times she had seen Lydia a little apart from the others, in mood if not in physical presence. The stage did not satisfy some far greater need in her than the admiration or even the love of an audience. And quite possibly she wanted what Alice had, more than Alice wanted it herself.

'Do you really think so?' Eliza asked. 'And then what will Alice do?'

Caroline smiled, but there was an edge of apprehension in it. 'Judging from what I have seen of her so far, whatever she wants to. And if the cost is high, she will have the courage to meet it.'

'Oh dear.' Eliza bit her lip. 'I was afraid that was what you were going to say.'

Half an hour later they were back rehearsing again. This time Caroline was taking notes for the lighting that would be required, as well as any further props to suggest a scene. They had bright limelights with them, and Joshua had shown her the equipment, and how to use it. It was a strange contraption with little taps to turn on the hydrogen and oxygen and a screw for rotating and raising the calcium oxide. Just at the moment all she wanted to do was make decisions where in the script the lights needed to focus, or be changed.

They began further towards the beginning. Joshua had done some rewriting. He had changed the situation to cut out Jonathan Harker's account of his travels in Transylvania, and given the speech referring to Renfield to Van Helsing instead. With the other character cuts, it worked far more smoothly.

Vincent was reading from the new script. Even though he described the reduction to insanity of a previously decent man, it seemed to Caroline to be without either honour or pity. She found her attention wandering, and was very much afraid that an audience would also. Was Alice's writing really so poor?

She looked at Joshua's face and saw his frustration. Alice had returned and was standing over at the far side of the floor, just below the stage. Her pale face and tight jaw betrayed that she also knew it was not working, but did not know what she could do to make it better.

Ballin stood up.

Vincent stopped, glaring at him. 'You have some superior knowledge of vampires, or of good and evil, to suggest how this could be better written?' he asked sarcastically.

'I have a suggestion how it could be differently played,' Ballin replied. 'But it would alter the character of Van Helsing somewhat.'

Vincent spread his arms wide. 'By all means. After all, what does Bram Stoker know about it? Or about anything?'

'We can't avail ourselves of his knowledge,' Ballin replied. 'At least not before Christmas, and we need a remedy rather sooner than that.'

'In what way would it alter Van Helsing, Mr Ballin?' Alice asked, cutting across Vincent.

Ballin moved towards the steps up to the stage. The lights shone on his coal-black hair and his unnaturally pale face with its powerful features.

'By giving him a little lightness,' he replied, glancing at her, then at Joshua. 'It is possible to be very serious about fighting evil without taking yourself so . . . pompously. Allow him a sense of humour, some eccentricity or talent other than his obsession with vampires.'

'That's the whole point of him.' Vincent was really angry

now. 'If you can't see that then you have missed the essence of the character.'

'That he has but one dimension,' Ballin concluded. 'You believe so?' Again he looked at Alice. 'I do not.'

Vincent opened his mouth to retaliate, and decided against it. He made an abrupt gesture and threw the script down on the floor, leaving its pages scattered.

Joshua was pale, the lines around his mouth deep-etched. He looked so weary Caroline longed to be able to help him, but could think of no way at all to do so.

Ballin climbed up the steps onto the stage, stopped to pick up the script and found the place where Van Helsing described Renfield.

'May I?' he asked.

Alice nodded.

'If you wish,' Joshua conceded.

Ballin began, using exactly the same words as Vincent had, but in a totally different voice. He was not Van Helsing using language to tell the audience how Renfield had caught flies and eaten them, or pulled the heads off rats to drink their blood, he was Renfield doing it in front of them. He buzzed, mimicking the flies. His hand moved so fast it was barely visible, as if he had caught the insect on the wing. The buzzing ceased. He put it to his mouth and crunched his teeth.

In the audience Lydia gasped and stifled a cry. Eliza Netheridge groaned. Mercy put her hand over her own mouth as if to prevent anything entering it.

Ballin went on. He described a rat, clicking his finger-nails on each other like rat feet on the floor. He wrinkled his nose, sniffing. He pounced on an imaginary rat, squeaking as the creature might, and made a movement as if tearing off its head.

Caroline felt her stomach clench and was glad she had not just eaten luncheon. In her mind's eye she could clearly see the miserable Renfield, reduced to an insane caricature of the man he had been, so in thrall to the vampire that he imagined he could survive only by such means.

Ballin handed the script back to Joshua and straightened up his back. The obscene pleasure left his face.

'There is nothing wrong with Miss Netheridge's words,' he said quietly. 'Although perhaps fewer of them are needed, if the actor portrays Renfield himself rather than Van Helsing telling us about him. Why should Van Helsing not be a man of imagination and empathy, even if it is for such a poor wretch as Renfield? That would enable us to see for ourselves the man's decline as Dracula's ascendancy over him strengthens through the story. It must be emotionally more powerful. And perhaps it also explains Van Helsing's greater ability to understand the vampire itself: an empa-thetic imagination?' He half made it a question, but the answer was obvious.

Joshua was smiling. He took the script back and made a brief note in the margin. 'You're quite right, Mr Ballin,' he said graciously. 'We can create a far more powerful image with imitation than description, and cut out a page or so of words. That way we may use the same device later on to show the cause of his decline. Thank you.'

Ballin bowed. 'It is my privilege to take part in your work, even if by so small a contribution.'

'It's not small,' Joshua replied. 'It is always difficult to reduce a cast drastically, and this helps us to conjure up from the audience the people we can't cut from the plot but have not actors to play them.'

They read through Lucy's death scene. The man she loved was one of the many characters who had been cut out. The scene could only be witnessed and felt by Harker and Van Helsing, and it lacked emotion. It was as if a stranger had died.

'We can dim most of the stage here,' Joshua said, frowning. 'Perhaps create more deliberate shadows.'

Alice was not happy. 'But we think Lucy has gone peacefully, to escape the pain she had here,' she said. 'We don't know yet what has really happened to her. Isn't this giving it away too easily?' Then she blushed at her boldness in challenging him.

'For heaven's sake,' Douglas said irritably, 'nobody's going to be so involved that it'll matter! It's a story, a piece of make-believe to entertain. I'm sorry, Alice, but it just doesn't matter.'

She ignored him entirely, as if he had not spoken. Caroline only knew that she had heard him by the pallor of her face and the muscles of her neck, which showed rigid above her lace collar.

'I don't think we should create more shadows,' Alice said to Joshua, as if they were the only two present. 'I think we should keep Mina here. After all, she is one of the strongest and most sympathetic characters, and she and Lucy were friends all their lives. Mina's grief can be ours. It wouldn't be difficult to write her in. I can do it this evening.'

Joshua hesitated only a moment. 'Good. We don't need much in the way of words, just the sight of her face. Give it to Mercy when you've finished.' He turned to Vincent, who was standing at the back of the stage looking elaborately bored.

'We'll have the bit where Lucy attacks the children. That needs more work on it. It's still awkward. We'll go through the scene in the script, and putting the stake through Lucy's body in the coffin. James, we'll have to see most of the horror of that in your face.'

They obeyed. Caroline watched and took notes until a late luncheon was served, then again all afternoon. They could not resolve the slow patches, or the technical difficulties, but continued into the search for Dracula after the destruction of Lucy's vampire form in the coffin. They put another excellent piece of mimicry into Van Helsing's part when he told Harker about Renfield's death and final release from his terrible state. Even in his very last moments, as his body contorted, he would not completely forget his lust for the life force in the flies and rats, so tight was the vampire's control over him.

They began to work on the first part where Dracula himself returns and attacks Mina, establishing the bond with her that would ultimately bring about his own destruction.

'It's coming,' Joshua said wearily, his voice cracking a little. It was nearly six o'clock in the evening and they were all exhausted. The snow was still streaming past the windows in the darkness, glistening briefly in the reflected light before they pulled the curtains closed.

He repeated the same belief again when he and Caroline were at last alone in their bedroom. The fire burned hot in the hearth, the guard set in front of it so no coals could fall out and set light to the carpet. It was warm; silent but for the rushing of the wind outside; and filled with a rare kind of comfort, as if they were uniquely safe.

'Is it coming, truly?' she asked him. She sat on the bed brushing her hair, finding the rhythm of the movement soothing.

He smiled. 'Alice is really quite good, you know. She's perceptive and she learns quickly.'

'Mr Ballin was brilliant.' She watched his face to read whether he minded or not. She saw only admiration.

'It makes me wonder if he is an actor himself,' he agreed. 'Or even a playwright. I didn't think of having Van Helsing virtually play Renfield as well, but as soon as he showed us it seemed obvious.'

'Will Vincent do it?' she asked with sudden anxiety. 'What if his vanity prevents him from taking the advice?'

Joshua smiled widely, almost a grin. 'You don't understand him yet, do you? He'll do it, believe me, and take credit for the idea. It's far too clever, too good a showcase for his talents for him to turn it aside. I won't have to persuade him, which is what you are afraid of.'

'Am I so easy to read?' she demanded, putting the brush down on the bed and letting her hair fall loose around her.

He looked at it with obvious pleasure. 'Yes, a lot of the time,' he answered. 'But only because I care enough to watch you.'

She smiled back at him, feeling more than the warmth of the room inside her, a safety deeper than the stone walls of this huge house on its hilltop defying the storm.

In the morning the wind had subsided but the snow was conspicuously deeper. Although the sky was clear overhead, there were dark clouds shadowing the land to the north and far out over the sea. No one bothered to say that there was worse to come: it was obvious to anyone who looked.

They began rehearsals again as soon as they had all finished breakfast.

'Today we'll go through it all, from beginning to end,' Joshua announced.

'It's only an hour long!' Vincent said, already short-tempered. 'For God's sake, how long can it take?'

'With your additions, all the damn day,' James snapped back at him. 'There won't be a fly left in Whitby.'

'There aren't any flies in the middle of winter, fool!' Vincent shot back at him. 'It's imagination. That's what acting is about.'

'Then we'll all try to imagine you're making a good job of it.' James was not going to be beaten easily. 'At least until Mr Ballin comes back again and shows you how to do it better.'

'A pity he hasn't shown you yet!' Vincent retorted.

'No doubt he will,' Joshua cut in. 'But until he does, let's see what we can do on our own. We'll start with thunder and lightning effects . . .'

Vincent stared around the room and then towards the windows. 'Probably unnecessary,' he observed.

'So is your remark,' Joshua said tartly. 'The coffin will be on the stage and dimly lit, and I will climb out of it. Then the lights will go out, and come on again to be moonlight. Caroline, can you manage that?'

'Yes,' she said immediately. She had practised with the limelight contraption and she felt more confident, but not as sure as she sounded. She too could act!

Joshua smiled. 'Good. Lucy will be sitting on the seat or by the shore. I will attack her . . .'

'Are we going to go through that?' Lydia asked. 'Please? We haven't done it yet?'

'Yes, I suppose we'd better,' Joshua agreed. 'Then Lucy at home with Mina and Harker. She is ill. Harker sees the bite marks on her neck. She gets worse and Mina cares for her. Dim lights to see Dracula at the window. He comes in and bites her again. In the morning she is far worse.'

'I thought Harker was supposed to be in Budapest?' James interrupted.

'He is,' Joshua answered. 'But since we have written so many characters out of it because we've no one to play them, we have to have him here. We've altered the story-line appropriately.'

James shrugged.

'Van Helsing arrives and tells Harker about Renfield—' Joshua went on.

'When do Mina and Harker get married?' James interrupted again. 'It's supposed to happen in Budapest.'

Joshua glanced at Alice.

'They'll have to be married before we begin,' she answered. 'I didn't think of that, but I can't see that it matters.'

'Good.' Joshua looked at his notes again. 'Lucy is attacked again and gets worse. We don't need to see the attack—'

'Yes we do,' Lydia was the one to interrupt this time. 'Otherwise it doesn't make sense.'

'No we don't,' Joshua told her. 'If we do it too often it loses impact. The audience can deduce that it happened. One really dramatic and powerful scene is better than two weaker ones.'

'They aren't that powerful,' Vincent pointed out. 'You need to be far more sinister. At the moment you look like a lover come up the garden ladder to elope. Or a burglar caught in the act!'

Alice was frowning. 'There is something else important we missed out—'

'You missed out,' Lydia corrected her.

'I missed out,' Alice accepted the rebuke.

'What?' Joshua was puzzled.

'Mr Ballin said that the vampire cannot come in unless he is invited. Someone has to invite him, and the audience needs to see that.'

'Mr Ballin says?' Vincent allowed his contempt to darken his voice. 'Since when has he been in charge?'

Alice blinked, but she did not retreat. 'The suggestion is a good one, Mr Singer, and that is all that matters. It is an important point that evil cannot come in unless we invite it. It is our choice.'

'None of them had the faintest idea what he was,' Vincent argued. 'Or did you miss that point?'

'Perhaps they should have known,' she countered. 'But it is naïve to imagine anyone is so good that they are immune to evil. Or perhaps it is a total lack of humility that makes one vulnerable?'

'Vincent wouldn't know anything about that,' Mercy remarked. 'Humility, I mean. He probably has no idea what you are talking about.'

'Neither have you, my dear,' Vincent said to Alice. 'This is supposed to be drama, not schoolgirl philosophy.'

Joshua drew in his breath. Caroline knew it was to defend Alice, but she spoke for herself before he could.

'I did not invent vampire lore, Mr Singer. I am simply quoting what Bram Stoker wrote. Since it is his book, and it greatly adds to the power of the drama, I wish to keep it.' She looked for a moment at Joshua, to make sure he approved, then turned back to face Vincent.

Joshua was amused. He tried to hide it, and failed.

'We will put it in, even if it requires an added scene,' he agreed. 'You are quite right. It makes moral sense, and for the audience we must have that. Then we will do Lucy's death scene, as witnessed by Mina. We will dress her in white and keep the light on her to suggest that Lucy is still innocent in appearance and still beautiful.'

Lydia smiled.

Alice ignored her.

'Then we will move to the scene where Lucy attacks the children,' Joshua continued. 'We haven't got any real children so let's see if it works to have Alice create children's voices for us – high-pitched and terrified.' He looked at Alice. 'You'll have to practise that. Then Lucy appears with blood on her mouth and face, and walks through the gravestones to return to her coffin.'

'How are we going to get gravestones on the stage?' James asked.

Joshua looked at Caroline.

'Eliza and I have found some very good old cabin trunks,' she replied. 'They are solid and about the right size, stood up on end. We can easily cover them in paper and paint on them appropriately. We can get some stones and a little bit of earth from the kitchen staff.'

'Very good,' Joshua said with satisfaction.

'We find Lucy's coffin in the crypt, empty,' he went on. 'We may have to condense this a bit: instead of finding it empty, have her in it, but serene and lovely, then empty again. It will have to be once only, for the sake of time.'

'It will be stronger if it is shorter,' Alice agreed. 'But we should see the terrible smile.'

'We will.' Joshua did not even think to argue. 'We'll see

Lucy as a vampire quite clearly, and the struggle that Harker and Van Helsing, and Mina, have to kill her. With lights we can make her seem to return to herself and be at peace. That is really the end of the middle act.'

'Bravo,' Vincent said sarcastically.

Joshua ignored him. 'Then we move into the beginning of the climax, the search for Dracula. We start to realise more clearly that Renfield's behaviour reflects Dracula's being nearby.' He looked at Vincent now. 'Van Helsing will recount that, with the mimicry,' he instructed, 'including Renfield's death, with appropriate sadness for Mina and Harker. We'll include his reference to rats and flies. I know that's a repeat of his previous references, but this time his manner will be different, and it should be a nice counterpoint.'

No one interrupted, but looking round at them Caroline saw that he had their complete attention. Not even Douglas Paterson objected, as if at last he were drawn into the story.

'Then we have the big series of scenes where Dracula appears and attacks Mina. The audience knows it, but Harker and Van Helsing don't . . .'

Eliza Netheridge was sitting next to Caroline. 'This is getting rather exciting, isn't it? I begin to understand why Alice cares so much.' She looked across at Alice, who was standing at the far side of the stage, her eyes on Joshua.

'Van Helsing realises the awful truth of Mina's condition when he places the holy wafer on her forehead and she screams with pain. It leaves a red scar,' Joshua went on. 'They corner Dracula, but he escapes.'

71

Eliza shuddered.

'Mina tells them that at sunrise and sunset Dracula has lost much of his control over her,' Joshua continued the narrative. 'Van Helsing hypnotises her and she says that when Dracula calls her – and he will – then she will have no power except to go to him, wherever he is, and whatever that costs her. She might well lie to them, or even attack. That should build a very real terror.' Joshua smiled. 'At that point we should have them on the edge of their seats. Then we have the climax.' He glanced at Caroline, then away again.

'This will call for some clear lighting to create the illusion of movement,' he went on. 'And then of a screaming wind and a snowstorm in the Carpathian Mountains. We may have the snowstorm given us by nature,' he added ruefully, 'but we must still make an audience realise that at this point it is also part of the story. Our three remaining characters are huddling together as it comes close to darkness, waiting for the coach with Dracula in his coffin returning to his native soil, which will regenerate his power. They have to drive a stake through his heart to destroy him for ever, or else he will destroy them. We have a little to do on the effects, and to make certain that all the necessary information is given without slowing up the action or breaking the sense of doom and terror.'

Vincent grinned. 'Actually it sounds quite good,' he said reluctantly. 'It might even be passable, by the time Boxing Day comes. Let's hope there is an audience.'

'If there isn't, we'll put it on for the servants,' Joshua retorted. 'Now let's get to work.'

They worked again in the afternoon. For a while the challenge of creating a story in which they could all believe overtook their personal differences. There was a spark of excitement in the air.

Caroline leaned forward in her seat as they put more movement into their positions on the stage. The play was beginning to come alive. She forgot she was sitting on a chair in a stranger's house in Whitby, working to make something good out of something poor. Bram Stoker's characters became people; the dark shadow of the vampire reached out and chilled them all, even in the sparse and critical audience.

Vincent was enthusiastic about Van Helsing's new and larger role. As Joshua had told Caroline, he grasped the chance to play Renfield as well. He did not do it exactly as Ballin had, but he did it slyly, at moments pathetically. In spite of herself, Caroline was forced both to be fascinated by it and moved. Renfield became not a device to further the plot but a real person, revolting and pathetic. Vincent Singer was Van Helsing, and Van Helsing in his portrayal was Renfield. The magic was complete.

When they changed the scene, stopping for a few minutes to talk about movements, Caroline turned to Eliza sitting beside her. She saw the awe in Eliza's face, the emotion still almost naked.

Aware of being looked at, Eliza coloured a little and smiled apologetically. 'I'm sorry, did you say something?'

73

'No. And please don't be sorry. You were caught up in it. So was I. It is the greatest compliment you can pay an actor,' Caroline replied.

Eliza looked startled. 'I suppose it is. You know, for a moment I believed it as if I were there. Do you suppose there really are people like poor Renfield?'

'I fear there are.' Caroline shivered. 'But I am quite sure that there are no actual vampires.'

'Actual?' Eliza stared at her. 'But such seductive art is real, isn't it! People who prey on one another, even who live by feeding on each other in some emotional way.'

'I think that is the whole point,' Caroline agreed. 'It would hardly frighten us if the danger were only imaginary. We jump at shadows the first time, and then we laugh at our own foolishness and feel silly, but happy that there was no substance to it. If at heart we know the evil is real, just not perhaps this time, then it is a completely different feeling.'

Eliza looked at her with anxiety. 'Should we be dealing with real evil at Christmas? Isn't it . . . inappropriate?'

'Isn't the good real?' Caroline asked simply.

Eliza swallowed hard, her throat tightening.

'I used to believe it was something of a fairy story,' Caroline went on seriously. Sarah's death came back to her, and all the others. She felt the horror again, imagined the pain and the violence behind the faces of people she thought she had known for years. It was as sharp as if it had been yesterday.

'Now as I get older and have seen more, I believe it is

real. We need redeeming so desperately. We need hope because without it we have nothing. If there is a God, then all the rest of the mercy and the renewal must be true also, even if we understand only a little of it, and nothing at all of how it works. We get so much wrong, make so many rules because it deludes us into thinking we have control of it. We don't, and we shouldn't want to.

'For heaven's sake, we are so limited!' she added with sudden ferocity. 'We need someone infinitely bigger and wiser than we are. But you cannot have good without also the possibility of evil, so if there are angels then there must be devils as well. If we are even remotely honest, we know that. So . . .' She looked at Eliza's face and wondered if she had already said too much. 'So in a way devils are good,' she finished. 'Because the reverse is true also. If we are reminded of evil, even supernatural manifestations of it, then we will believe in and love the good even more.'

Eliza was smiling. She put out a hand very tentatively at last, then with more assurance, resting it on Caroline's arm. 'My dear, you are a remarkable woman. I could never have imagined that watching a group of actors working would have taught me something I so badly need to know. Thank you so much.' Then as if embarrassed by her frankness, she stood up and excused herself to go and speak to the cook about dinner. 'I fear we shall have to be a little more sparing with our rations than usual,' she added by way of explanation.

Caroline thought that the cook would have noticed for

herself that the snow was impassable, but she only nodded agreement.

On the stage they were proceeding with some of the later scenes; Vincent Singer was elaborating on Van Helsing's intellectual brilliance.

Caroline watched Joshua, and knew he did not like it. She agreed with him. Glancing at the faces of those who were watching, they were bored as well.

Mr Ballin came in silently, bowing briefly to Caroline, and to Alice and Lydia Rye, who were both sitting in the audience. Douglas Paterson ignored him but Ballin did not see anything untoward.

Caroline watched Joshua standing on the stage holding the script in his hand. She could see he was troubled. He had asked Vincent to make more of Van Helsing's character, his humanity. But now that Vincent was adding depth to him, it was not coming alive, and he was searching for something better before he interrupted. They could not afford the time or the emotional energy for tantrums, and Singer was crucial to the drama.

Vincent continued, making Van Helsing seem a genius.

Alice sat wincing, looking more and more troubled.

Finally Joshua interrupted. 'Vincent, this doesn't work. It's taking up too much time, and half of it is irrelevant.'

Vincent stared at him. 'I thought you wanted Van Helsing to be more of a character? As Miss Netheridge has written him, he's flat and even tedious. And more importantly, he's no match for Dracula. How many times have you told us that a hero has no validity if the villain has no menace and no power? Surely the reverse must be true also?'

'Yes, it is,' Joshua conceded. 'But telling us he is clever doesn't convince—'

'What do you want?' Vincent demanded. 'I'm an actor, not a conjuror or a contortionist. You want the music halls for tricksters!'

'It's too many words,' Joshua said flatly. 'We stop listening.'

Ballin walked over towards the stage. 'No one cares for a man who boasts of his achievements,' he said quietly but very clearly. 'And we have to like Van Helsing, even if we do not always understand or approve of what he might do, perhaps until after he has done it; then we see the necessity.'

Vincent started to speak, and Joshua held up a hand to silence him.

'What do you suggest?' he asked Ballin.

'Let him solve a problem, a difficulty of some sort,' Ballin replied. 'Then his quick thinking, his knowledge and improvisation will be evident, and useful. He will not need to boast; in fact he will not need to speak at all.'

'Oh, bravo!' Vincent applauded. 'Such as what? I'm sure you must be overburdened with examples.'

Ballin thought for a moment. 'Well, the use of light and mirrors is always interesting,' he replied. 'Especially with vampires, who traditionally have no reflection.'

'We already know who the vampire is.' Vincent dismissed it with a degree of contempt.

Ballin ignored him. 'Van Helsing could arrange mirrors

77

that reflect from each other, magnifying light and sending it around corners. Vampires are creatures of the shadows. At least to begin with, Dracula does not wish to be exposed.'

'Brilliant,' Vincent said sarcastically. 'Then we lose all the tension because we defeat the poor devil right at the beginning. How is it we let anyone fall victim to him? Are we all just blazingly unimportant?'

Ballin was still unperturbed. 'We do not succeed because Lucy is bitten outside, in the night before Dracula ever enters the house, but Van Helsing doesn't know that. Nor, at the beginning, does he know the depth of the vampire's seduction. Lucy moves the mirrors, just as later Mina will lie, and even become violent, when Dracula calls her.'

Joshua was smiling slowly.

Ballin continued, 'Later Van Helsing would suggest an alarm to warn them all if anyone enters Mina's room through the window. A chemical device, of magnesium dislodged by the movement so that it lands in water. It will give off a brilliant white light, which could be seen by anyone watching the window from another part of the house.'

'And they don't come running to the rescue because . . . ?' Vincent asked, but his voice was now interested rather than dismissive.

Ballin smiled very slightly. 'Because Mina has drugged their wine. That is already in the story. Again, clever as we are, we have underestimated the strength of the vampire's hold over our minds.'

Reluctantly this time Vincent agreed.

'Good,' Joshua said firmly. 'Now there is the problem of lighting the scene where we peer into Lucy's tomb in the crypt. I haven't worked out yet how we can do that so the audience can see. The sense of shock and dawning horror is crucial.'

'Any ideas for that?' Vincent asked Ballin.

'Do not show the audience,' Ballin answered.

'Oh, superb!' Vincent jeered. 'What shall we do? Recite it to them in the rash of words you are so much against? I'm sure that will frighten them out of their wits! Very dramatic.'

Ballin kept his patience. He smiled, as if amused at Vincent's contempt. 'Most emotions are the more powerful for being shown through the characters we identify with,' he said calmly. 'Open the tomb with a creak, a sigh of hinges, and let us see the horror dawn on the faces of Van Helsing and Mr Harker, even Mina, whom we admire so much. Let us see her grief for her friend Lucy. Perhaps you need an additional scene earlier on so we may observe how fond they are of each other? We will know that something is terribly, hideously wrong, but for a space of seconds time will stand still and we will not know what it is. Our imaginations will fill it in with a score of different abominations. Then one of you may say that the tomb is empty.' Ballin spread his hands in an elegant gesture, his pale fingers catching the light.

They went on discussing, adding to and taking out, and by the end of the afternoon they were exhausted. Caroline and Joshua went up to their room, Caroline grateful for an hour's respite from the subject before they all met again for dinner.

But when they were in the bedroom and the door closed she could see that Joshua was still worried. He certainly would not rest as she had hoped.

'It's not working,' he said bleakly, standing at the window and staring out at the light catching on the pale blur of snowflakes in the darkness beyond. 'Not yet.'

She bit back her impatience. The disappointment in his voice pulled at her emotions and crushed the irritation she had felt mounting inside her.

'I thought Mr Ballin's suggestions were very good,' she said, knowing she risked making him feel as if he should have thought of them himself. Just now she believed rescue was more important than its source.

He turned to face the room, the lines around his mouth deep etched, his eyes pink-rimmed. 'They are,' he agreed. 'But they are only cosmetic. There is still a lack of cutting edge to it. Dracula isn't . . . isn't terrifying. We can feel the horror, but not the evil.'

She wanted to be helpful but nothing came to her mind that was honest, and he did not deserve to be patronised with false comfort. 'I'm not certain if I know what evil is, on stage,' she said unhappily.

He pushed his hands into his pockets. 'Ballin is right: we won't see it in itself. It will become real to us when we see the effects in others. I wish I could think how to show that.'

'Who is this Mr Ballin?' she asked curiously. 'He seems to know a lot about vampires, and about acting. How can he? *Dracula* was only published this year.'

'I've no idea who he is,' he replied, walking over towards the bed and lying down, hands behind his head. 'I could sleep until tomorrow,' he said. 'Except that I can't afford to.'

'Mina,' she said with certainty.

'What about her?' He was confused.

She turned towards him. 'Jonathan Harker is an usual sort of hero, but he's . . . I don't know . . . a bit cardboard, terribly predictable. He isn't like any real person I know because he has no faults, no vulnerabilities – unless being a cracking bore is a vulnerability. It isn't, is it?'

He smiled. 'Not on stage. Bores don't feel hurt, they just drive everyone else to drink. What are you getting at?'

'We don't really care about Harker,' she explained. 'We know he's good, but we don't care. Van Helsing is a know-all. We need him to defeat Dracula, and we believe he's going to. In fact I suppose we take it for granted. But Mina is good, and vulnerable too – I mean, really good. She cares about other people. She's brave but she has enough sense to be frightened as well, and later on when the holy wafer burns her, we know that Dracula has got to her. She is the one we need to care about, and see her slowly pulled further and further down. I would mind terribly if anything happened to her that even Van Helsing couldn't save her from.'

He sat up. 'Would you?'

'Yes. Yes, I would.'

81

He leaned forward and kissed her, gently and for a long time.

'Then we shall let them think Mina will not survive,' he said at last. 'Thank you!'

At morning rehearsal the following day Ballin attended again. Now he was quite open about his suggestions and Alice was eager to adopt them. Douglas seemed less displeased, and Caroline noticed that when Lydia Rye was not on stage playing the character of Lucy, quite often they stood together. They did so awkwardly at first, but then with increasing ease. They might have been commenting on the play and its progress – Caroline was not close enough to hear – but the unspoken communication between them was quite different. She had learned from Joshua the difference between text – the words on the page that actors spoke – and subtext – the emotional meaning that they conveyed and, if the acting were any good, that the audience understood. For Douglas Paterson and Lydia the subtext was that they were increasingly drawn to each other. Alice either had not noticed, or else she had, and was not as disturbed by it as one would have expected.

Did she believe she could undo it as soon as Lydia left? Was she so confident of herself, or of Douglas's love for her? Or had it perhaps to do with her father's wealth and the opportunities that it would offer Douglas in the future? Was she really so shallow? So vain?

Caroline found herself hoping very much that that was

not so. She liked Alice. She was highly individual, and reminded Caroline increasingly of her own daughter Charlotte, another young woman full of impractical dreams.

Or was it that Alice reminded her of herself? What kind of a woman with any sense would abandon a respectable and financially safe widowhood in order to marry a Jewish actor seventeen years her junior? Perhaps Charlotte had inherited her wilful streak from her, and Caroline should be the last person to fault her for it?

Now on stage the drama was beginning to form a coherent whole. At last Joshua himself was acting, not merely reading his part and watching the situation and the details of others. The entry of Dracula made all the difference.

Even so, Ballin still made suggestions. They were going through the whole script in order of playing, beginning with the storm and the landing of the coffin at Whitby.

Very carefully Caroline dimmed the lights, then increased them slowly as the coffin lid opened, hesitated a moment, and then Joshua emerged. She almost stopped breathing as he uncurled his body and stood up, his face wreathed in a terrible smile.

There was a gasp from Alice sitting close in the front row, and Mercy gave a little shriek.

'Ah!' Ballin said with satisfaction. 'But one small suggestion. May I show you? It might be simpler than trying to explain.'

Joshua's jaw tightened, but he stepped aside. 'Of course.'

Caroline dimmed the lights and began again.

Ballin climbed into the coffin and lowered the lid. There was a moment's silence. Everyone was watching. Very slowly the lid rose again, perhaps two or three inches then long, white fingers emerged, curling like talons, feeling around as if in search of something.

'Oh God!' Mercy breathed, her own hands flying to her face.

The coffin lid continued to open very slowly. A full arm was visible. Then still carefully, noiselessly, Ballin climbed out and stood up, his head peering from side to side.

There was no need for anyone to comment; the difference was too clear to require it.

Caroline found herself tense when they resumed, picking up the action as Dracula crept up on Lucy as she sat on the bench overlooking the sea. They went through the motions of the attack, but again it lacked the knife-edge of terror. After the power of Dracula's emergence, it was an anticlimax.

'The book says a bench, a park seat,' Joshua said unhappily. 'It's awkward. It's just physically clumsy.'

'You are right,' Ballin agreed. He turned to Alice. 'Have you any better ideas, Miss Netheridge? Something less . . . pedestrian? Certainly something less impossible to relax back against.'

'Relax?' she said in astonishment. 'She is attacked by a vampire just risen from the grave!'

'No, no, no!' Ballin shook his head. 'She is seduced Miss Netheridge. We have seen him walk from his coffin but she has not. We watch the horror, helpless to prevent it. That is your tension. Never forget it. We know he is something hideous, risen from the dead, but to her he is a lover, bewitching her, filling her dreams.'

'Ugh!' Alice shuddered, but there was no denial in her face. On the contrary, her eyes were bright with a kind of luminous excitement.

From the back of the room, Douglas Paterson looked at her with distress mounting into anger.

'Perhaps it isn't the path above the cliff at all,' she suggested, watching Ballin. 'What if she has gone to the graveyard to pay her respects to a dead father, or mother?'

'A gravestone?' James said in disbelief. 'You want her seduced on a gravestone? Miss Netheridge, that is . . . vulgar, even blasphemous.' His face showed his distaste very plainly.

Alice blushed, but she did not retreat. 'It is her neck he bites, Mr Hobbs. I was not imagining an overtly . . .' she swallowed, '. . . sexual scene. I am surprised you were.'

Now James blushed scarlet.

Ballin smiled. 'An excellent idea, Miss Netheridge. I assume you had in mind one of the taller stones. If she were to lean back against it all the symbolism is perfect, the suggestion without the gross detail.' He swung around to Joshua. 'Do you not think so too, Mr Fielding?'

There was only an instant's conflict in Joshua's face, then the resolution. 'Of course,' he agreed. 'It might be difficult to make something suitable. For now we can use one of the upended trunks.'

It took ten minutes to find such a thing and prop it up,

with weights at the bottom so it would stand. They replayed the scene, and suddenly it was transformed. The gravestone worked perfectly, lending height and allowing Joshua to raise his arms with the shielding cloak. The audience could imagine anything they wished. When he moved back, slowly, as if sated, Lydia leaned half collapsed against its support.

From the audience Mercy gave almost involuntary applause. It was as if she were so moved that for a moment her professional enthusiasm overrode her personal need to be in the limelight.

Dracula's first entry to the house, with Mina's invitation to him to come in, had to be done several times. It was mostly in order to place the lighting in exactly the right position so he stood first in dramatic shadow, and then emerged out of it, from a figure of menace to one of increasing charm, even grace. The final time, even Mr Netheridge could not help but be fascinated. He had come in quietly and was watching from the back.

'Aye,' he said grudgingly. 'It's gripping, I'll grant you that.' He turned to Alice. 'You've done well, girl. I begin to see what you're on about.'

She smiled and said nothing, but the pleasure was bright in her face. She looked across at Ballin, and he gave a tiny nod of acknowledgement. It was so small that Caroline, looking across, barely saw it.

The scene with Van Helsing acting Renfield worked superbly. For once, Vincent was excellent. He would not have admitted it, but he copied almost exactly what Ballin had done, and his own sense of timing asserted itself. The result was both chilling and pathetic, and very real.

By the time they came to Lucy's death they were all swept along in the story. Even James, as Jonathan Harker, displayed a sensitivity Caroline had not seen in him before. Mercy's grief as Mina reduced the audience to a throat-aching silence, and from Eliza, who had returned to watch also, a quick dabbing of her eyes.

Luncheon was cold meat sandwiches, pickles, and then hot apple pie with cream, all served in the theatre.

'I think we should see more of Harker and less of Van Helsing in the tomb scene,' Mercy said suddenly. She had just finished the last of her apple pie and was reaching for the excellent white wine that had been served with it. 'It would improve the pace. Van Helsing is the intellect, Harker is the heart and the courage of the pursuit. Apart from Mina, of course.'

'Of course,' Lydia answered. 'Actually the core of the scene is Lucy. She is the one who has become a vampire. And we still haven't decided exactly what we are going to do about the children.' She looked at Joshua, then turned to Ballin. 'Perhaps Mr Ballin, who seems to have been sent here by the storm to solve all our problems, will be able to answer that for us as well?'

'We are reduced to illusion,' he said thoughtfully. 'We have no way of physically representing a child, at least not one alive. Alice—' For the first time he used her given name.

'That's stupid!' Douglas cut across him. 'She is nothing like a child. She's a full-grown woman, at least in appearance.'

Ballin's face tightened with anger, whether for himself or for Alice it was impossible to tell. 'She is also quite a passable actress, Mr Paterson,' he said very softly, very precisely. His voice was oddly cold, as if there was some threat in it. 'We can make a dummy, something of pillows, with the appearance of arms and a head. I'm sure Mrs Netheridge's maid can give us a dress that will do. The minds of the audience will create for them what they expect to see.'

Joshua gave a sigh of relief.

Douglas snorted with contempt, although Caroline was certain that it was actually frustration.

'The master of delusion and deceit, aren't you!' Douglas spat the words.

It was Alice who sprang to Ballin's defence. 'Stagecraft, Douglas. I'm sorry you don't know the difference. It is causing you to be unnecessarily rude to our guest.'

'He is not our guest,' Douglas reiterated. 'He is a stranger who landed on the doorstep out of the storm, melodramatically, asking for help, and has been aping Dracula ever since.'

'Don't be ridiculous!' she said angrily. 'He told us what happened. His carriage overturned and broke a wheel in the snow. He won't be the only person stranded in this weather. What on earth would anyone do except invite him in, especially at Christmas? What would you have done? Told him there was no room at the inn?'

'Invite the vampire into your house,' Douglas answered, his own voice louder and more strident. 'He told you himself: evil can only come in if you invite it.'

Alice paled a little. 'Anyone can come in only if you invite them,' she said, glaring at him. 'Don't tell me we've done this so well you actually believe in this vampire stuff?' She tried to laugh, and failed. It came out as a gasp of breath, with no humour, not even any conviction.

'I believe in evil, and stupidity,' he said bitterly.

Her eyes raked him up and down. Her lip curled a little. 'Don't we all?'

'Of course we do,' Lydia moved closer to Douglas's side. 'If we didn't before, we should do now.' She faced Alice. 'You are fortunate to have the love of so fine a man, Miss Netheridge. I think he is something like Jonathan Harker, brave and modest, not knowing how to fight evil because he has none within himself to understand it.'

Alice was even paler now. She started to say something, then changed her mind and walked away.

'Perhaps you'd like to attack the children again after we've finished lunch?' Joshua suggested with an edge of sarcasm that was breathtaking. 'Just pretend you have the dummy in your arms. Leave it in the shadows. Drop it, if it seems right to you, and then come forward to Harker and Van Helsing.'

Caroline put her hands over her face and pretended she was somewhere else, just to give herself time to re-gather her strength.

* * *

The crypt scene, and Lucy's final scene as a vampire, went quite smoothly. They moved into the last act: the hunt for Dracula. Vincent overplayed Van Helsing's mimicry of Renfield, but the third time through he added some details. These were so vivid, and actually tragic, showing Renfield as a man once decent, a victim of the vampire, that Joshua told him very firmly to keep it in. If the play ran five minutes longer, then so be it.

'It's not necessary,' James protested. 'We're ten minutes over time already. We'll lose the audience.'

'No we won't,' Joshua told him. 'It's a superb piece of acting . . .'

'We're here to entertain, not show off,' Mercy said defensively. 'Vincent's just trying to impress Mr Netheridge. He's looking for another lead in the London West End.'

'On that performance, he deserves it,' Joshua admitted. 'But it's important to the play. He makes Renfield matter to us . . .'

'Renfield's trivial, a plot device,' James said with disgust.

'He's a plot device that works extremely well,' Joshua said gravely. 'His degradation from decent man to fly- and rat-eating lunatic shows us more clearly than any words what the power of the vampire is. Through Van Helsing we watch him die, but, for an instant, return to the man he once was. This is the only time we see that, and we understand how far he fell. If we're not frightened of Dracula after that, then we are truly stupid.'

James drew in his breath to argue, then let it out again.

He was actor and dreamer enough to know the truth of what Joshua said.

They followed the script through to the end. They even tried the effect of the lights to create the illusion of a snowstorm and cut down the words used to describe the last chase of the coffin through the mountain pass as the sun sank in the west, and they killed Dracula in its last rays. The unearthly scream as the light faded and the curtain came down drew a moment's total silence, and then a roar of applause.

'It will work,' Joshua said simply. 'Thank you for your ideas, Mr Ballin. You have helped us enormously. Without you we might never have succeeded.'

Ballin bowed, smiling. 'It was a great pleasure,' he said. 'A very great pleasure. Miss Alice, I think you have a happy future ahead of you.'

'Thank you,' she whispered, her eyes shining.

Dinner was quiet. Everyone was tired and there were no more problems to solve. Only the script, much amended, had to be learned by heart so there were no mistakes, no hesitations. Everyone was happy to retire early. There was a lot of studying to be done. In fact, for several of them a new copy of the script would be made, without the scratchings out and margin notes. Some found writing it out themselves an excellent way to commit it to memory.

Caroline wrote out the script as well, not every word, but the key phrases that prompted where she was to change the lights. The whole script to be followed for prompting would be with Alice. Her parts on stage were only a few words here and there: a servant or a messenger. It would not be difficult to fill all the roles. The lights were crucial.

Joshua was sitting at the small desk in the bedroom and Caroline was on the bed, reading her cues over again when she remembered a note she had written hastily and left on the stage.

'I'll just go and get it,' she said, slipping her feet off the bed and standing up. 'I won't be long.'

'Shall I get it for you?' he offered.

'No, thank you.' She walked over to him and touched his cheek lightly. 'You're busy.' She looked down at his half-written page. 'There's another hour's work at that. I'm not afraid of vampires in the dark. I'll be back in ten minutes or so.'

He smiled and turned back to the desk. She was right, he knew it would take at least another hour or so to complete.

Caroline went out onto the landing and down the stairs to the main hall. The lights were always left burning low, but quite sufficient for her to move swiftly towards the passage to the theatre. The hall seemed even more magnificent in the shadows: the ceilings higher, the chequered marble floor bigger, the stairs sweeping up on either side disappeared in the dark corners where they turned and curled back to the gallery above.

The long passage to the theatre was even darker, leaving the distances between heavily shadowed, the outlines of pictures barely visible. She walked briskly. There were no chairs or jutting tables to bump into, not even the vase of bamboo now.

She turned the first corner, then the second, looking for the next lamp along. Then she tripped over something and pitched forward, landing hard on the floor on her hands and knees. She got up slowly, shaken and bruised. How could she have been so clumsy? She turned to see what she had fallen over, and at first did not understand what it was. She was in the shadow between the lights and it looked like a pile of curtains dropped on the ground.

Then as she stood dazed, her heart pounding, her eyes became more accustomed to the heavier shadow. It was more clearly a man lying crumpled on his side, his legs half folded under him. A drunken footman? What on earth was the stupid man doing here?

She bent to shake him, then she saw the long handle of the broom slanting upwards. Except it wasn't a broom – at least, it was only half of one. The brush was missing, and the shaft ended in the man's chest. She felt the light and shadows blur and swim as if she were going to faint. She closed her eyes for a moment, then opened them again. It was not a footman, it was Ballin. His eyes were open and his mouth was open, as if he had screamed when the makeshift spear had struck him. She had no doubt whatever that he was dead.

Should she scream for help? It seemed ridiculous to scream now, deliberately. Added to that, her mouth was as dry as if she had been eating cotton wool. She should stand up, control herself, make her legs walk back up the stairs to tell Joshua. Please heaven no one come along this corridor in the meantime.

Her legs were wobbling. It was all she could do not to fall again. What had happened? Was there any imaginable way it could have been an accident?

Don't be absurd, she told herself, crossing the hall as silently as she had the first time, a world and an age ago. Nobody takes the head off a broom and spears themselves with the handle by accident. In fact, it must have been sharpened or it wouldn't penetrate the skin anyway.

She reached the stairs and clung onto the newel post, climbing up hand over hand, pulling and balancing.

She was at the top of the stairs. She reached her bedroom door and opened it. She saw the light on Joshua's brown hair, shining on the fair streaks in it.

'Joshua . . .'

He turned around slowly, the pen still in his hand. Then he saw her face.

'What is it?' he said huskily, throwing the covers off and starting up. 'Caroline!'

'Someone has killed Mr Ballin.' She gulped, struggling now not to sob, not to let her knees buckle. He was beside her, arms holding her.

'I tripped over his body in a dark stretch of the corridor to the theatre,' she went on. 'Before you ask, yes, I am sure he was killed . . . murdered. He has been stabbed through the chest with the broken-off handle of a broom. You could say . . .' She gulped again and the room swam and blurred in the corners. 'You could say down through the heart with a stake.' She wanted to laugh but it ended in a sob.

He was guiding her to the bed, still holding her.

'Have you told anyone else?' he asked, his voice unsteady.

'No. I . . . I thought of screaming, but it seemed so stupid. We must tell Mr Netheridge. Do you know which is their bedroom?'

'No. I shall call one of the servants. They should inform him.' He glanced at the window, then back at Caroline. She was sitting on the bed now, and he still held both her hands. 'We will have to deal with it ourselves.'

'Joshua, it's murder!' she protested. 'We can't just . . . just deal with it, as if it were some kind of domestic accident!'

'And who's going to walk through that snow to fetch the police?' he asked very gently.

'Oh . . . oh.' She took a deep breath. 'Yes . . . I see. How stupid of me. We'll have to . . . oh heaven!' Now she leaned against him as her body began to shake. 'That means one of us must have done it.'

He touched her hair gently, pushing the long strands away from her face.

'I'm afraid it does. There won't be any more strangers out in the night coming here, or anywhere else.' He let out a long, shaky breath. 'I'll go and get one of the servants. The butler, I suppose. He'll call Mr Netheridge. At least we must get a little decency for the body.' He took a step.

'Joshua!'

He turned. 'You stay here. Perhaps you had better not let anyone else in.'

'Put a blanket over the body, if you like,' she told him. 'But you'd better not move it until someone has looked at it. It's a murder. We have to find out who killed him.' She smiled bleakly and it felt like a grimace. 'I've been around rather a lot of crime, one way and another. Thomas is a policeman, if you remember.'

'We can't leave it there until the thaw,' he protested. 'We'll have to find a better place, somewhere cold. But yes, perhaps one of us should take a very careful look at it first. I don't know who – Netheridge himself, I suppose. It's his house. You know I have the odd feeling that Ballin would have been the best person to take charge, if the dead man had been anyone else.'

He looked very pale. For a ridiculous moment she thought what a disappointment it was that they would hardly be able to put on the play now. It really had become very good.

'Yes,' she agreed. 'He was very able. I'm . . . sorry he's gone.' It sounded so inadequate, and yet it was all she could think to say.

'Stay here,' he repeated, then he went to the door and out.

It was nearly half an hour later when Joshua returned. Caroline insisted on going down with him to the withdrawing room where the rest of the company was gathered. All had dressed again, but hastily, and none of the women had bothered to pin up their hair. Everyone was clearly shocked and frightened. James and Mercy sat together on the couch, he holding on to her hand. Douglas Paterson stood behind the big armchair in which Alice was hunched up. Her face was white and she was clearly distressed. Lydia Rye sat alone, as did Vincent Singer.

Eliza sat close to where her husband stood with his back to the fire, which had been stoked up again after having been allowed to burn almost away. The huge stained-glass window made the room look like a church.

Joshua and Caroline took places on the other sofa.

Netheridge cleared his throat. 'It seems we have a very ugly tragedy in the house,' he said with deep unhappiness. 'No doubt you all know by now that the stranger, Mr Ballin, has met with a very sudden death.' He glared at Vincent, who had seemed about to interrupt him. 'We don't yet know what happened, whether it was some sort of accident, or worse. If anybody has anything they can tell us about it, now would be the time to do so. Obviously we can't call a doctor, or the police. We have no way of getting out to do it, and they have no way of coming to us, until the weather improves. No doubt they will clear the roads as soon as they can.' He looked around the group hopefully.

No one answered him.

'Who was Ballin?' he demanded. 'He appeared out of the night and asked for shelter. We gave it to him, as we would. Who knew where he came from? Did he talk to any of you? Did he say who he was going to visit here in Whitby? Why? What does he do? Where does he live? We don't know him!' His glance embraced Eliza, Alice and Douglas Paterson.

'For heaven's sake, we don't know him either,' James said heatedly. 'We don't even know anyone else in Whitby.'

'Well, why would anybody kill him?' Netheridge asked.

'He was an objectionable, interfering and arrogant man.' Douglas pulled his mouth into a thin, hard line. 'He was not difficult to dislike.'

Caroline lost her temper, which was something that occurred very rarely indeed. She had been brought up to believe ladies never did such a thing.

'Mr Paterson, this man has been run through the chest with a broom handle. The fact that you did not care for him is irrelevant. Unless you are saying that your dislike was sufficiently intense for you to have murdered him? And I do not think that is what you mean. Somebody here obviously had a far deeper hatred or fear than that. One does not take another human being's life violently, in the middle of the night, without a passion that has slipped out of all control. Your resentment of his generosity to work with Alice, and to help her believe in her ability, is surely not of that order, is it?'

There was a stunned silence.

Douglas was white to the lips. 'Of course it isn't!' he said savagely. 'How dare you say such a thing? The man was arrogant, and probably a charlatan, but I didn't do anything to him at all. Look at your fellow players. It has to be one of you.'

It was Vincent who answered, his eyes wide in disbelief.

'One of us? Why, for God's sake? It was this house he came to. It is just conceivable that he had heard Mr Netheridge was entertaining his friends with a group of professional actors in his daughter's drama, but he told us it was a surprise. Even if it were not, how would Ballin know who we were? One has to assume it was someone here he came for, someone he expected to find.'

Netheridge's face flushed dark. 'I've never seen the man before, or heard of him!' he protested. 'Neither has anyone in my family, and that includes Douglas Paterson.' He was horrified, but he was also afraid. His big hands clenched at his sides and he started to take a step forward, then changed his mind.

'There is no point in trying to lay blame on each other,' Caroline said as levelly as she could. 'We would all rather it were someone who broke in from outside and had nothing to do with any of us, but that hope would be childish and help nothing. No one has come or left. Either it was a sudden quarrel so violent that it ended in death, or else he already knew someone here – either who lives here or who is visiting – and an old quarrel was renewed. It doesn't matter. I doubt anyone is going to admit to either.'

'Maybe he attacked someone, and they had to defend themselves?' Eliza said shakily. 'That would mean it wasn't their fault, wouldn't it?'

Caroline looked around them all slowly. For a moment her heart was pounding and her mouth dry with the hope that that could be true. Then the dead man, beyond all further hurt, would be to blame. Even as she thought it, she knew such a hope was false, but she could not give it up easily.

'No one looks to be hurt,' she said at last. 'No one is dirty or torn, as if they had been in a fight for their lives. And surely if it were so, they would now admit it?'

'One of the servants?' Mercy said immediately.

Caroline gave a little shrug. 'Why would Mr Ballin be in the corridor to the theatre in the middle of the night, attacking one of the servants with a broken-off and sharpened broom handle?'

'How do you know it was sharpened?' Douglas challenged her.

'Because it wouldn't have speared him if it were blunt,' she said with weary patience. 'This is not a play, this is real. It has to make sense. Anything that doesn't can't be true.'

'We must wait for the police.' Netheridge took command again. 'Until then there's nothing we can do. Please, everyone, go back to bed and get whatever rest you can. Douglas and I will go and move the poor man so that none of the servants find him. They're a sensible lot, but this will distress them, naturally. I think it would be a good idea if we merely say that Mr Ballin was taken ill and died. Time to amend that when the police come.'

Caroline rose to her feet. 'You can't do that!'

'I beg your pardon?' It was a rebuke, not a request.

'Of course he can,' Douglas said sharply. 'You've had a shock, Mrs Fielding. Let your husband take you upstairs again and perhaps you have a headache powder . . . or something . . .' He tailed off lamely.

Caroline remained where she was. 'You can tell the servants whatever you think is best to keep some sort of calm in the house,' she said to Netheridge, ignoring Douglas. 'But Mr Ballin was murdered. I quite see that you have to put his body somewhere more suitable than where it is, and perhaps not tonight in the dark. If you bolt the door to that part of the house it can be done in daylight, but it would be most unwise to do it alone . . .'

'My dear Mrs Fielding, it will be unpleasant, but there is absolutely no danger whatever, I assure you,' Netheridge said patiently. 'He is a perfectly ordinary man of flesh and blood, and the dead do not hear us. There are no such things as vampires, or the undead—'

'Of course there aren't!' she cut across him angrily. 'But he was murdered. Anyone moving him before the police get here may be accused of altering the evidence.'

'What evidence? We can't leave him there, woman! He'll . . . smell! The natural—'

'I'm not suggesting we leave him there,' she corrected him. She was beginning to tremble. 'But we need to be there, all of us, or at least several. One of us did that to him. We don't want the police to accuse any of us of moving something that would have indicated guilt.'

'Such as what, for heaven's sake?' Netheridge pretended to be outraged, but understanding was already beginning to show in his eyes.

'Such as proof that Ballin knew them, or that there was some quarrel between them,' she answered. 'Something on his clothes or his person to show who was the last one to see him alive. All sorts of things are possible, either to find there because they were left accidentally, or on purpose by someone wishing to implicate somebody else; or not to find, because they have been removed.'

'She's right,' Mercy said incredulously. 'But how on earth do you know these things? Who are you?'

'I am Joshua's wife,' Caroline replied. 'But I have a son-in-law who is a policeman and he has solved dozens of murders – scores. On occasion, a case has touched my own family . . . Please . . . let us use sense as well as compassion. We'll all go together, in the daylight, when we can see the body, the floor around, anything that can tell us what happened. We need to protect ourselves from unjust suspicion by the police, as well as anything else.' She stopped, swallowing hard, her mouth dry.

'You are quite right, of course,' Netheridge agreed more calmly. 'Thank you. Fielding, perhaps you would come with me while I lock the door from the hall to the corridor. As Mrs Fielding points out, we need to take the proper care to be above suspicion. I shall see you all at breakfast at the usual hour. Until then, please take whatever rest you can.'

Caroline sat up in bed waiting for Joshua to return. It seemed like ages, although it was probably little more than five minutes before he came in and closed the door. He looked very shaken.

'It's locked,' he said quietly. 'I'm sorry you had to see that. Are you going to be all right?' He looked at her anxiously, trying to read beyond the calm words with which she replied.

'Did you look at him?' she asked then.

He sat down on the edge of the bed. 'Only briefly. I suppose Netheridge wanted to make sure you hadn't had a nightmare, or something. I'm afraid it's definitely Ballin, and as you said, someone killed him. That sort of thing couldn't have happened by any kind of accident.' He touched her hair, then her face. 'I wish I could have protected you from this. I knew there'd be difficulties, quarrels in the cast, but I never imagined it could end in violence.'

'Of course you didn't,' she said, surprised at how calm she sounded. 'It's probably to do with Netheridge, not us, but we must be prepared to deal with whatever happens.' She smiled bleakly. 'You know I'm really very angry. We had finally made a decent play of it, and now we can hardly perform it, in the circumstances. Added to which, I liked Mr Ballin, odd as he was.'

No one had slept well, but they were all present at breakfast, which was a silent and unhappy meal. When it was completed, Mr Netheridge announced that it was time to carry Ballin's body to an appropriately cold room on the outside wall of the house. This was often used for the storing of meat, when the ice house would have been too cold.

Obediently they rose and followed him across the hall, then waited while he got the key and opened the door to

103

the corridor. He turned the lock, swung it open, and – after taking a deep breath – set off at a brisk pace. They followed obediently, Mercy and Lydia a step or two behind the rest. For the first time that Caroline had observed it, they seemed to cling to each other as if they were the friends that Mina and Lucy were in the play.

They rounded the last corner and saw the stretch of linoleum floor ahead of them; the pool of dark blood on the floor; the long shaft of the broom handle, sharp, scarlet-ended; but no corpse.

Netheridge stopped abruptly.

Douglas Paterson swore.

Mercy screamed, loud and piercingly sharp.

Lydia quietly slid to the floor in an awkward heap.

Douglas swivelled round, saw her, and went to her anxiously, calling her name and trying to raise her up in his arms.

James went to Mercy, catching her hands, which she was waving around. 'Stop it!' he said loudly. 'It's all right! He's not here. There's no danger at all.'

'No danger?' she shrieked. 'He was dead, someone murdered him, with a stake through the heart and now he's not there any more, and you say there's no danger? Are you mad, or stupid? I told you there was something wrong with him, terribly wrong. He came here out of the night and the storm, just like the one that brought Dracula's coffin ashore.' Her voice was getting louder and higher-pitched. 'He knew everything about vampires, more than we did, more than Bram Stoker did. He was dead and locked in, and still he escaped. Except he wasn't dead, you fool! You can't kill him, he is the undead.'

White-faced, Eliza turned to Caroline.

Caroline stepped forward. 'Mercy!' she said abruptly. 'You are not helping anyone by being hysterical. If you really want to step out of reality into Mr Stoker's book, then for goodness' sake live up to the character you chose to play. Mina would never have been so peevish and cowardly, and she was faced by a real vampire who was determined to kill her. Mr Ballin, poor man, is dead and can do you no possible harm, even if he wanted to. Take hold of your emotions and stop making such an exhibition of yourself. We need to think very clearly what to do if we are to defeat the evil that is here.'

'Evil!' Mercy repeated the word with a loud wail. 'Then you don't pretend there isn't evil here!'

'Stop shrieking!' Caroline commanded. 'I would be delighted to have an excuse to slap your face. If you insist on giving it to me, I shall take it, I warn you.'

Mercy fell instantly silent.

'Thank you.' Caroline's voice was tart. She turned to Netheridge. 'There is no point in our standing here. Clearly the body has been moved. Since there is no one in the house except us and the servants, you had better find out if one or two of them came here and found him, and in decency put him somewhere else. One thing is absolutely certain: he did not remove himself, either as a man, or as a bat or a wolf, or anything else supernatural. If you don't want all the maids in hysterics, and possibly the footmen as well – or, worst of all, the cook – then you had better be very circumspect as to how you do it.'

'Yes,' he agreed, as if he had thought of it himself. 'Of course.' He turned to Joshua. 'I'm sorry, but in the circumstances I don't believe there is any point in your continuing to practise for the play. I . . .' He shook his head. 'Just at the moment I hardly know what decisions to make about anything. Please . . . look after yourselves. Do as you please. I'm sorry, but clearly it is quite impossible for you to leave, or even to walk outside. The snow must be a couple of feet deep, and it is bitterly cold. There are books in the library, quite a good billiard table . . .' He did not bother to finish.

Caroline felt sorry for him. The party he had planned with such care for his daughter had collapsed in a tragedy no one could have foreseen. Now instead of celebration he had a crime, and a group of strangers in his home without a purpose.

She stared at Joshua, then at Netheridge. 'Mr Netheridge.'

He turned towards her, simply out of a host's good manners. His face was weary and he looked ten years older than he had when he welcomed them to his home. 'Yes, Mrs Fielding?'

'Alice has written a play that we have all worked on, particularly she. We will perform it one day; if not here then somewhere else. Possibly even in London, at the very least in the provinces. Considering how much he contributed to it, we could do it in memory of Mr Ballin. Our time and her efforts have not been wasted.'

He swallowed, sudden emotion filling his face. It was a moment or two before he could master his voice.

'Thank you, Mrs Fielding. You are a generous woman, and brave. I hope one day that will be possible.' Then, before he embarrassed himself by display of his vulnerability, he made his excuses and left.

One by one they all went: either to their bedrooms, the billiard room, the library, or the room set apart for letter-writing with desks, inkwells and ample supplies of paper.

Caroline walked away from the dining room and up the stairs to go back to her bedroom. Then she changed her mind and went to the window seat in the long gallery from which she could see across the snowbound countryside. The hill fell away, covered by trees now bending under the weight of last night's new fall. Some of them looked precariously close to breaking. There was no mark on the landscape of human passing: no wheeltracks, no footprints. It was impossible to tell how deep the snow lay, except that all the smaller features, rocks, low walls or fences had disappeared. They were alone.

Far out towards the sea more clouds were piled up, ominous and heavy grey. There was worse weather to come.

She realised as she sat there that they must solve the crime themselves. They could not remain here day after day knowing nothing, doing nothing. One of them had killed Anton Ballin. They had to find out who it was, and be strong enough to deal with the answer, and certain enough to act together, whatever that answer was. Of course it must also be done without anyone else being killed. A person who would spear Ballin to death might not hesitate to do the same to anyone who threatened them.

How? It seemed unimaginable from the slight vanities and squabbles they had shown on the surface. They were no more than pinpricks to the self-esteem: a lesser part on the small stage, not even any money involved, or any critical review to care about. It made no difference to anyone's career.

And yet someone had cared about a loss or a fear so intense that they had driven a broom handle through a man's body. Why? What was it that lay below a surface that appeared so normal? They had all been deceived, ignorant, walking a razor's edge across an abyss, and never thinking to look down.

She shivered, although it was warm in the house. Fires burned in every room. Candles blazed. Food was plentiful and excellent. There were servants to attend to every physical need. What lay hidden behind such apparent ease that was so terrible it killed?

How could she find out, and so discreetly that she did not get herself killed in the process? If she had any sense at all, she would take very great care indeed. For a start, she would tell no one what she was doing, and that included Joshua. In fact more than anyone else, she absolutely mustn't tell Joshua.

She was speaking to herself as if she had accepted that identifying the murderer was her responsibility. But who else was there who could possibly do it? None of them had any experience of murder, except herself.

Douglas Paterson was possibly guilty. He had loathed Ballin, and made no secret of the fact that he thought Ballin was deluding Alice that she had talent when she had not. Not that it was a talent Douglas was willing for her to use. It would mean her leaving Whitby, where his future lay. If she did not marry him, then perhaps he did not have a future – not in the way he had imagined, and intended. Charles Netheridge was a very wealthy man indeed. The house more than attested to that, quite apart from his frequent and large investments in the London theatre. Alice was his only child.

That was why he had been willing to invite an actor of Joshua's fame and quality up to Yorkshire for the whole Christmas period, and pay his expenses and those of his company, on the understanding that he would stake them next London season.

Who in the company could have hated Balling so much? He was a stranger to all of them – what danger could he present? Surely nothing in the four days since he arrived had given birth to a passion so violent it had ended in that terrible act in the corridor?

He must have known one of them before? How did he threaten that person now? Had he come to seek revenge for some old wrong?

Caroline had been watching the sky without thinking about it. The dark clouds over the sea were closer now, and heavier. A gust of wind stirred the bare branches, sending piles of snow falling off into the deep drifts beneath.

Was it possible that Ballin had not been the intended

victim? In the uncertain light of the corridor could the killer have mistaken Ballin for someone else? He was tall, but so was Vincent Singer, and James Hobbs. With his back to the candlelight, would such a mistake be possible? They might not have spoken. Ballin's voice was distinctive.

Netheridge was of average height, and broader than any other man here. He walked quite differently. Douglas Paterson was a good height, but he had not the practised grace or elegance of Ballin.

She could not believe there had been such a mistake.

The sharpened broom handle was a very carefully prepared weapon. It had been created, not used in any spur-of-the-moment anger or self-defence. Nobody possessed such a thing, never mind carried it around with them in the middle of the night, unless they had attack in mind.

Was it possible someone really did believe in vampires? Was anyone so crazy? Surely not? They were actors; they played all sorts of parts, real and fantastic. They could take up roles as they stepped onto the stage, and discard them again as they left it. She had seen Joshua as everyone; from pensive heroes like Hamlet to blood-soaked tyrants like Tamberlane; lovers, as Antony was to Cleopatra; or philosophers; cynics or wits as any number of protagonists in Oscar Wilde's works. None of them was the real man she knew.

Was Mercy's fear a vain woman's pretence to get anyone's attention, or could she really fear the 'undead'? People have all kinds of religious or superstitious beliefs. The fact that the body had apparently disappeared now made that fancy less ridiculous. Or had someone hidden it to cause precisely that fear?

Possibly. But that would have been as an afterthought, not a reason to murder Ballin.

Had they intended to meet there in the middle of the night? It was ridiculously unlikely as a purely chance encounter, surely? Which meant that Ballin knew this person in a way that made him keep such a tryst.

Why was the body moved? Because there was something about it that would give away the truth of the crime. What could that be? Either something of the identity of whoever had killed him, or something about Ballin's own identity that would betray who he had known well enough for them to hate or fear him with such passion.

Whom could she ask for help? The only person she trusted without question was Joshua. However, he would be fully occupied trying to keep up morale and sensible behaviour among the cast, especially now that there would be no performance, at least in the foreseeable future. He would have to find them something to do, to keep at bay, hold them together as a group rather than allowing old jealousies to surface in the present that might result in near hysteria, when things would be said that could not be mended.

Someone must find out who had killed Ballin, and prevent the wrong person being accused. She, Joshua and the rest of the players were strangers here in close-knit Whitby. Who would suspect even Douglas Paterson, never mind Netheridge himself, when they had the perfect scapegoats in a group of strangers, and actors at that?

She must squash down her own emotions and think clearly. What would her son-in-law, Thomas Pitt, do? Ask questions to which there would be precise answers, which she would then compare. With luck, a picture would emerge, even if it were merely of who was lying and who was telling the truth.

Maybe she would be better equipped if she knew more about the people. For a start, she would definitely need the help of Eliza Netheridge to speak to the servants. She did not imagine for an instant that any of them had killed Anton Ballin; why on earth would they? But they should be eliminated all the same.

She found Eliza in the housekeeper's room. After waiting several minutes for her to complete her conversation, she followed her as she walked back to the main part of the house.

'I was wondering if I could be of help in any way,' Caroline began. 'I don't know if you have told the servants or not.'

Eliza looked very pale in the white daylight reflected off the snow outside. The fine lines around her eyes and mouth were cruelly visible.

'Charles said I should not,' she replied. 'He has told them that Mr Ballin was taken ill. We were going to say that he had died and we had placed him in the coldest storeroom until the authorities could come, but of course now we don't know where he is.' She stopped and turned to Caroline, her face tight with misery. 'Where on earth do you think he could be? Why would anyone move him?' She was trembling very slightly. She seemed to want to say more, but some discretion or embarrassment prevented her.

Caroline longed to be able to help her. She looked frail and a little smaller than she had seemed only yesterday. Had she been going to ask Caroline if she had any belief in the supernatural, and then was afraid to seem ridiculous?

'Perhaps to frighten us,' Caroline answered with a very slight smile. She meant it to be reassuring, and was suddenly anxious in case Eliza imagined it was out of mockery, or amusement at her superstition. 'And they've succeeded,' she went on hastily. 'We are all unnerved by it. But honestly, I think it is probably for a more practical reason, such as that if we were to look at the body more closely we might learn something that would indicate which one of us killed him.'

Eliza looked close to tears. She stood still and stared ahead of her on to the huge hall, with its magnificent decoration and its oil portraits of various Yorkshiremen of note. They were the choice of a rich man who had local roots, but no ancestry of which he was proud.

Eliza gazed at them one by one on the furthest wall, her face filling with dislike.

'I don't even know who they are,' she said softly. 'Charles's mother chose them, and there they hang, watching us all the time.'

'There aren't any women,' Caroline observed.

'Of course not. They're councillors and owners of factories who gave great gifts to the poor,' Eliza told her. 'I think they look as if they parted with their money hard.'

'They look to me as if they had toothache, or indigestion,' Caroline answered. 'Perhaps they were very bored with sitting still. I don't suppose they could even talk while they were being painted.' Then another thought occurred to her. 'Didn't any of them have wives, or daughters? A woman with a red or yellow dress would brighten up this hall a lot.'

'Charles's mother chose them,' Eliza repeated. 'Nothing has ever been changed since her day. Charles won't have it. He was devoted to her.' There was defeat in her voice, and a terrible loneliness, as if she were a stranger in her own house, unable to find anything that was hers.

'What about a painting of you?' Caroline suggested. 'And surely he would want to have one of Alice? She has a lovely face, and if she wore something warm in colour, full of pinks or reds, she would draw the eye away from all those sour old men.'

'I don't think so,' Eliza said, but clearly turning it over in her mind. 'But you know, I think I'll try. Tell me, Mrs Fielding, was Alice's play really any good? Please don't make up a comfortable lie. It would not be kind. I think I need a truth to cling on to, even a bad one.'

'Yes, it was,' Caroline said honestly. 'And by the time we had worked on it and rehearsed it that last time, it had become really excellent. There were some moments in it that were unforgettable. Above all, it touched on the real nature of evil, not of attack by the supernatural, but seduction by the darker side of ourselves. Mr Ballin was very clever, you know, and Alice could see that. She had both the courage and the honesty to learn.'

'Thank you. That comforts me a great deal, although I don't think Douglas will allow her to write another, or indeed to have that one performed properly, by people with the talent to understand it. It is . . . it is a great pity that it will not now happen this Christmas.'

'Yes, it is,' Caroline agreed. 'But please don't give up hope for the future.'

'Douglas doesn't like it. He won't allow it. He has said so.' There was the finality of defeat in her eyes and in the downward fall of her voice.

'Are you sure?' Caroline asked with a growing fear inside her. Was that perhaps the reason for Ballin's death? It would not only ensure that the play was not performed for Alice, but also be a kind of punishment for Ballin because he had been the one whose suggestions had brought it to life with its depiction of the fear and reality of evil.

'Oh, no!' Eliza breathed the words more than said them. 'He wouldn't . . .'

'Who wouldn't?' Caroline asked, knowing Eliza had no answer.

Eliza gave a tiny gesture of helplessness, and said nothing.

Caroline went into the hall, leaving Eliza a few minutes of privacy before the next demand on her time from one servant or another with their domestic issues.

She found all the cast in the large withdrawing room, sitting around in various chairs reading or talking quietly to each other. Douglas Paterson was there as well, listening to Lydia describing something to him. Caroline could not hear the murmured words but she saw the animation in Lydia's pretty face, and the delicate gestures of her hands as she gave proportion to the scene in her recollection. Douglas's eyes never left her. He was oblivious of everyone else in the room, including Alice talking with Joshua at the further side near the window.

Vincent, Mercy and James were all reading, grouped close together as if only moments before they might have been involved in some discussion. None of them looked up as Caroline came in. Suddenly she felt the same sense of exclusion that Eliza felt. She was here, this was the right place for her to be, and yet she did not belong. She had never stood on a stage in her life, never played a part so convincingly that a vast sea of people in the shadow of an auditorium listened to her words, watched her face, her movements, while she held their emotions in her hands, moved them to laughter or tears, to belief in the world she created with her presence. It was a magical art, a power of drama she was not gifted to share.

She turned away again and went back out into the hall with its grim portraits. Maybe she would never be a part of their art, but she had a skill they did not have. She would find out who had murdered Anton Ballin, and why.

She continued to struggle with the problem of even where usefully to begin. She had no authority to ask questions, no physical material to examine – not even the body at the moment, although that would no doubt reappear quite soon. It could not be far away because no one could possibly have left the house with it.

She could have searched Ballin's luggage, but he had brought nothing with him but a small hand case. Why not? Presumably he had had cases with him in the carriage that had been overturned and broken its wheel? Possibly they were too heavy to carry in the snow. What had he brought? At the very least a razor and a hairbrush? A clean shirt and personal linen? It meant that there was little of his own that she could look at to get some sense of the man: quality, use, place where they were made or bought, anything that told of his personality or his past.

What would Thomas have done? Well, for one thing – being a policeman – he would have had the authority to be able to question people.

She would probably learn nothing if she went to Ballin's room and searched, but she would be remiss not at least to try. She could even ask one of the servants if they had noticed anything. Better to look herself first.

She knew where the other members of the company had rooms, so she could deduce which Ballin's must be. The family slept in a different wing. Of course it would be possible to misjudge and end up in Douglas Paterson's room, but she thought that was a little separated from the main guest wing and easy enough to avoid. It was really a matter of not being caught by a housemaid.

Ballin's turned out to be a very pleasant room overlooking the garden. It was not as large as the one she shared with Joshua, but then Joshua was the most important guest. Ballin had been no more than a stranger in trouble, given shelter because the storm had left him stranded.

Was that all he had been?

She stood at the window and stared out at the snow-smothered lawn and the trees so heavily laden as to be almost undistinguishable one from another. Not a soul had passed that way in the last twenty-four hours, at the very least; perhaps not since the first storm struck.

She looked around the surfaces of the dressing table and the tallboy, the two chests of drawers. There were the hair-brush, razor and strop she would have expected, but no pieces of paper, no notes. She turned to the bed. It was slightly crumpled, but not slept in. The sheets were still tucked tightly at the sides. He had lain on it, but not in it.

She looked at it more closely, but again there were no written clues tucked between the folds of the sheets, or under the pillows.

She tried the drawers, and found only clean, folded under-wear, presumably mostly that lent to him by Netheridge. There were two shirts hanging in the wardrobe, and a jacket, also lent to him. There was nothing in any of the pockets. He had died wearing his own clothes: the black suit and high-collared white shirt in which he had arrived.

Where else was there to look?

There was a carafe of water on the bedside table, and an

118

empty glass. She could not tell if he had drunk anything because the glass was dry, but the carafe was little more than half full.

Caroline bent and looked to see if anything could have fallen onto the floor and slid under the bed. She lifted the heavy drapes, but found nothing, not even dust.

Lastly she looked at the coal bucket by the fire, and into the cold grate. If she had received a note to keep an appointment at night, secretly, she would have burned it. It was the easiest and surest destruction.

There was a faint crust of grey ash at the edge of the cinders. It had burned through and curled over, subsiding on itself. If she touched it at all, even breathed on it, it would collapse into a heap of ash. However, she was sure it had been a small piece of paper, such as one might use to write a note. There was no way to prove it. Even trying to would destroy it.

So Ballin had received the invitation, or the summons. Whoever it was from had gone prepared, carrying the weapon.

She stiffened as she heard footsteps outside in the corridor, and a maid's laughter. Would they come in here? Surely Mr Netheridge would have told them not to?

Or would he? Would he even think of it? He had probably never experienced anything to do with murder before. Very few people had. Caroline must do something before they disturbed anything, and then tell him.

She opened the door and came face to face with one of the housemaids, a tall girl with dark hair. The girl gave a little shriek and stepped backwards sharply.

'I'm sorry,' Caroline apologised. 'I wanted to make sure that nothing had been disturbed here. Mr Netheridge requests that you do not come into this room, in any circumstances. Do you understand?'

'Yes . . . yes, ma'am,' the girl said obediently, looking puzzled.

Caroline wondered whether she should ask Eliza to lock the door. But if she did that, the maids would wonder where Ballin was. Perhaps it could be explained as an infectious disease? Or would either curiosity or compassion still get the better of someone?

How much did it matter? There was nothing in there, except the curled-over ash remnant of a note, which no one could read now anyway.

'Thank you.' She smiled at the girl and then came out into the passage, closing the door behind her. She would find Eliza immediately and apologise to her for giving her staff orders, and explain to her the necessity.

Eliza looked surprised. 'I . . . I never thought of it,' she admitted. 'Mr Netheridge thought it better not to tell them anything, which I find very difficult. They will not see Mr Ballin, and they know perfectly well that he cannot have left. No one could.' She bit her lip. 'If they ask me, and the butler certainly will, what should I say?'

'I think perhaps that Mr Ballin is ill and must not on any account be disturbed. We are not certain if what he has might be contagious. But I would add that only if necessary.'

'Then why do we not feed him?' Eliza said reasonably.

'Even the sick need to eat and drink, and also have their bed linen changed.'

'Perhaps we may know the truth before such an issue is obvious,' Caroline said gravely. 'If not, then perhaps it will be time for the truth we have.'

'Where is he?' Eliza's voice dropped to a whisper.

'Well, he has not returned to a mysterious coffin somewhere,' Caroline assured her. 'But we do need to know as much of the truth as possible, for our own safety, and to prevent any further tragedies.'

'Will it prevent tragedy?' Eliza looked at her candidly. 'One of us here in this house must have killed him. There's no one else, and there is no possibility whatever that it was suicide or accident. He could not have done that to himself, even I can see that. Who carries around a broom handle carved to a spear point in the middle of the night, unless they intend to kill someone?'

'Nobody,' Caroline agreed. 'And we all know that. We will all be afraid, and wondering. Do you think there is any chance we can forget it and carry on as normal until the snow thaws and the police can arrive, and ask all the same questions, except days later when we don't remember it as sharply?'

'No. So what can we do?'

'There are three things we can agree about,' Caroline answered. 'Who had the ability to kill him: that is, the means? Who had the opportunity: in other words where were we all at the time it must have happened? And who would want to: who believed they had not only a reason, but no better solution?'

Eliza frowned. 'Can we do that?'

'We can certainly try,' Caroline said with more conviction than she felt. 'We know that Mr Ballin was killed some time after we parted to go to bed, and before I went down again to fetch the note I had left behind on the stage.'

'What times were those?' Eliza asked. They were standing on the landing at the top of the stairs, talking quietly. No one else seemed to be around. Housemaids were busy, footmen must have been in the servants' quarters and would come only if the doorbell rang, which at the moment was unlikely. Kitchen staff would be busy preparing luncheon for the household, which – including servants – was well over twenty people.

'We went to bed at quarter to eleven,' Caroline answered. 'I went down to get my note just before midnight.'

'An hour and a quarter, roughly,' Eliza said. 'Everyone would be in their bedroom. How does one prove that?'

'Well, I know where Joshua was and he knows where I was,' Caroline reasoned. 'You and Mr Netheridge could account for each other, as would Mercy and James.' She stopped, seeing a shadow in Eliza's face. 'What is it?' she said more gently.

'Charles and I do not share a bedroom,' Eliza confessed, as if it were some kind of sin. She looked deeply uncomfortable. She seemed to be struggling for an explanation, but no words came.

'I'm sorry,' Caroline apologised. 'In a house this size of course you would not need to. In later years I did not share a bedroom with my first husband.' She smiled briefly; the memory no longer hurt. 'He was very restless. I share with Joshua because I'm happy doing so, and also we do not have the means to do otherwise, most of the time, especially when we are travelling.'

Eliza smiled and blinked. 'You are very generous. It must be an interesting life, going to so many places, meeting people, performing different plays. You can never be bored.'

'I'm not.' Caroline wondered how much of the truth to tell. 'But I am quite often lonely, because I am not part of the cast.'

Eliza looked amazed. 'But you are. You are involved.'

'Not usually. This is in many senses an amateur production . . . it was. We were to make our own scenery, and I was taught how to work the lights. In an ordinary professional production there is no work for me, except sometimes to help Joshua learn his lines. I speak the other parts to cue him. Otherwise I have nothing in particular to do, and we are away from home a lot.'

'But you are happy,' Eliza said, smiling. 'I can see it in your face, and in the way you look at him, and he at you.'

Caroline wanted to thank her, make some gracious acknowledgement, but she found a sudden rush of gratitude brought tears to her eyes and a tightness to her throat that made it momentarily impossible. She had risked so much in marrying Joshua: the horror of her family; the

123

outrage of her former mother-in-law; the loss of most of her friends and certainly any place in the society to which she had been accustomed all of her earlier life. She had been respectable, and financially safe. Now she was neither. But she was certainly happier, and she was very aware that Joshua loved her in a way Edward Ellison never had.

She also realised that Eliza Netheridge had never experienced those gifts. Even now she felt a stranger in her own house, as if her mother-in-law still watched her every choice with disapproval.

Caroline made a sudden, rash decision. 'Eliza, I wonder if you can help me. We may at the very least be able to make certain that some among us could not have killed Mr Ballin. I imagine it could not have been any of the servants, but let us save them from police questions and suspicion by making certain ourselves. I have no authority and no right to ask them, but you do. If you are careful, and precise, you may be able to find some sort of proof that clears them all. Especially if you promise them that whatever they were doing, there will be no blame in this instance. You may need to tell them that there has been something very unpleasant occurred, and it is absolutely necessary that they tell the truth, whatever that may be.'

Eliza took a deep breath, but she seemed perfectly steady. 'Yes, of course I can do that,' she said with determination. 'I shall begin immediately. Will you speak to your own people?'

Caroline smiled at the thought that the players could be seen as 'her' people. 'Yes. I'll begin with Mercy and James. That should be easy enough.'

But it was not. She found Mercy in the writing room busy with what looked like a pile of letters. Caroline was quite blunt about what she was asking, and her reasons. She had already decided that an attempt at deviousness would be highly unlikely to fool anyone.

'Between about half-past ten and midnight?' Mercy repeated blinking rapidly. 'I was in my bedroom, reading a book for a little while, then I went to sleep. You can't imagine I killed Mr Ballin. I wouldn't have the strength, apart from the . . . the violence of mind.'

'No, I didn't really think you did,' Caroline agreed. 'But I have to ask everyone, or else it will look as if I think those I do not ask could be guilty.'

Mercy smiled. 'I can see how that would be very awkward. Why do you want to know? The police will ask all those questions anyway. Why are you bothering?'

Caroline had already prepared what she meant to say. 'Don't you think it would be much less unpleasant if we can tell them some of us could not be guilty, before they have to ask? You never know what else they may enquire into, once they start.'

Mercy looked appalled.

'Not that it would be criminal,' Caroline went on. 'Just private.'

'Of course. Yes, you are absolutely right.' Mercy smiled

with considerable charm, and a degree of honesty. 'I under-estimate you, Mrs Fielding. I apologise.'

'Think nothing of it,' Caroline said airily, convinced that Mercy would do that anyway. 'Will James say the same thing?'

'Ah . . . well.' Mercy cleared her throat. 'That's it, you see. He was restless and he couldn't sleep. He said he was going to rehearse somewhere where he wouldn't disturb me. So, no, he wouldn't – not exactly the same thing, that is. It would mean the same, of course.'

'"Rehearse",' Caroline repeated. 'Are you avoiding saying that he went back to the stage?'

Mercy was perfectly still. 'Well . . .' she breathed out, '. . . I don't know where he went, do I? I was here. He may have gone to the billiard room. There would probably be nobody else there at that hour.'

'Did he say where he was going?' Caroline pressed.

'I don't think so.'

And that was all she could learn. She knew that persisting with Mercy would only make an enemy of her, and she would learn nothing more. And of course if she did not know for certain where James had been, then in reverse, he did not know where she had been either. That sort of testi-mony covered both people, or not. She thanked Mercy and went to look for James.

She found him in the billiard room alone, practising sinking the balls into the pockets around the table. She asked him where he had been at the time Ballin had been killed.

'Probably asleep in my bed,' he answered, putting the

billiard cue down across the table and staring at her. 'Why? Do you think I killed him?'

It was a far more aggressive answer than Caroline had expected, and it was interesting, as if he had foreseen the question and was prepared for it. Perhaps he was a better actor than she had given him credit for.

'I find it difficult to think of any of us doing it,' she replied. 'But the police may not have the same trouble. They don't know us, and to them we are a band of actors, travelling people with no roots and no respectable profession. And it is either one of us who murdered him, or one of the highly respectable Yorkshire people, townsfolk of Whitby most likely, whom they have known for years. What do you think they will be disposed to believe, James?'

His face blanched. For a moment he held onto the edge of the table as if he needed it for support.

'I think you take my point,' she said quietly. 'Mercy said you took your script and went out of the bedroom to practise, so as not to disturb her. The natural place to do that would be the stage. Is that where you went? If you did, you had better say so now. To lie about it, and get caught later, could be seen as damning.'

'I ... er ...' He blinked and shook his head, as if he were plagued by flies buzzing around him. 'I ... went to the stage, but it was cold and rather eerie there by myself. I decided not to bother, and I brought the script back and sat in the library. I didn't really want to rehearse so much as think of some way of making my part more heroic at the end. Ballin wasn't in the corridor then, I swear. I could hardly have failed to see him if he had been. Not if he was lying on the floor, as you say.'

'No,' she agreed. 'Thank you. I don't suppose you asked a footman to bring you a drink, or anything?'

'In the middle of the night?' He raised his eyebrows. 'I've got more sense than that. I don't want to be on the wrong side of Netheridge.'

She believed him. 'Thank you.'

'Mrs Fielding?'

She was almost to the door. She turned. 'Yes?'

'Who the devil was Ballin? Does anyone know? And where's his body gone to?' His face was still white in the pale daylight of the room.

'Someone must know who he is,' she answered. 'You don't sharpen a broom handle into a dagger to kill a stranger in the middle of the night, especially when you are all snowed in with each other.'

He put his hands over his face. 'Oh God! And the body?'

'I have no idea. Have you?'

'Me? No!'

'I thought not. Thank you, James.'

Vincent Singer was no more help. Caroline went to him next because it was the encounter she least looked forward to. She had little confidence that she could persuade him to talk, still less that she would trick him into saying anything he did not wish to, certainly not to reveal anything that would betray a vulnerability on his part.

She found him in the library, reading Netheridge's copy of Gibbon's *The History of the Decline and Fall of the Roman Empire*.

'Decay always fascinates me,' he observed, putting a piece of paper into the book to mark his place before closing it. 'You look troubled. Are you also afraid that Ballin is perched upside down in the rafters somewhere, waiting for nightfall to come and suck our blood?'

'I think he is far more likely to rot in the warmth, and attract rats,' Caroline said tartly.

He gave a long sigh. 'What a curious woman you are, all sweetness and respectability one moment, and violent imagery of the charnel house the next.'

'If you think that is surprising, then you know very little of women,' she retorted. 'Especially respectable ones. We usually only faint to get out of a situation we find embarrassing. I am surprised so many people believe it. Except, of course, those who lace their corsets too tight.'

'How extremely uncomfortable, and faintly ridiculous,' he replied. 'Since you appear to think I knew that, you did not come to inform me. What did you come to say? You have a look of purpose about it. No doubt it is grim.'

'Extremely. The police will come and investigate Mr Ballin's death when the snow thaws. I think it would be very much pleasanter for us if we could solve the mystery surrounding it before then.'

Vincent's eyes widened. 'Really? And how do you propose to do that? I do remember you saying, several times, that your son-in-law was some kind of policeman. Did you take lessons from him?' He made no attempt to hide his sarcasm.

Caroline sat down in the chair opposite him. 'If you disagree, I am perfectly happy to see if we can clear everyone else, Vincent. It may be one of the servants, although I think that is very unlikely. Or Mr Netheridge, of course. Whom do you think the police will suspect? Mr Netheridge, owner of the coal mine and the jet factory and philanthropist to half the country, or a group of London actors here to perform *Dracula* for Christmas?'

Vincent stared at her, his face pale and tight as he realised immediately the truth of what she said.

'You have a tongue like a knife, Caroline,' he observed, but his voice was shaking, in spite of his usual inner control. 'I can't prove where I was at the time he was killed, which was obviously after we all said goodnight, and whenever it was you went back to the theatre.'

'Midnight,' she told him.

'In bed, but no one can prove it for me. Thank God I won't be the only one in that situation.'

The next person Caroline saw was Douglas Paterson. She found him on the landing, staring out at the snow as she had done a short time ago. He turned as he heard her foot-steps. He looked withdrawn and anxious.

'Good afternoon, Mrs Fielding,' he said, almost without expression. 'Not long till dark again. Do you think we'll have more snow tonight?'

She stood beside him and looked at the sky. The light

was fading quite rapidly. It was barely past the shortest day of the year, but there was considerable colour in it. Banners of cloud streamed across the west and the red of sunset blushed on the snow.

'No, I don't,' she answered. 'I think we might even get a thaw soon, at least enough to allow people to reach us, perhaps by Boxing Day.'

'You can't put on that play now, you know,' he said with just a trace of satisfaction.

Caroline was caught with an intense desire both to protect Alice's dreams, and to deflate this pompous young man with his edge of cruelty.

'Not here,' she agreed. 'At least certainly not this Christmas. But she has made such a good job of it that I think we may wish to perform it some time in the provinces, or even in London. After all, *Dracula* is a most popular work all over the country. We could always bring it back to Yorkshire some more appropriate time.' She saw his face pale and smiled at him sweetly. 'Knowing how you love Alice and want her to be happy, I hope that is of comfort to you.'

He looked back at her with a fury that he was momentarily helpless to express.

'I am hoping we may forestall the police, at least to some extent,' she continued. 'They are bound to ask us all where we were when Mr Ballin was killed. Some of us are fortunate enough to have been with someone else at the time, and therefore our whereabouts are known.' She saw the anger turn to satisfaction in his eyes.

'I was with Miss Rye,' he said instantly.

There was nothing funny in their situation; still she could not help allowing her eyebrows to rise as if in horror. 'Really?' she said in a breathless whisper. 'And will Miss Rye be willing to say that publicly, do you suppose? I doubt Alice will be amused, and Mr and Mrs Netheridge will be most displeased indeed.'

He blushed scarlet with embarrassment and real, deep outrage.

'Your mind is most . . . deplorable, Mrs Fielding!' his voice shook. 'I dare say it is the company you keep.'

'I was with my husband, Mr Paterson,' she replied, angry in turn now. 'Or do I mistake you, and you had a chaperone you omitted to mention? Alice herself, perhaps?'

He swallowed hard, his face still burning. 'No . . . no, we were alone, in the morning room. We . . . we were discussing Alice's love of the theatre, and Miss Rye was assuring me that it is not nearly as glamorous as Alice assumes. She herself is weary of it, and envies Alice's opportunity to settle down to a happy married life in a respectable society, with a husband and family.'

And money, Caroline thought, but she did not say so. It occurred to her how much more suitable for everyone it would be if Lydia married Douglas, and Alice came to London with the players. Lydia's roles could be easily enough filled by another aspiring actress, and Alice would be an asset to the writing and producing side of the business. More importantly for both of them, and for Douglas, they would be happier.

'It seems as if each desires what the other has,' Caroline said more gently. 'Perhaps they should exchange places.'

'I can't marry an actress!' Douglas said in horror. But even as the words left his lips there was a change in his attitude, a new brightness in his eyes. The anger seeped out of him as if by magic.

'Well, she isn't an heiress, of course,' Caroline agreed. 'But that has its advantages as well. There is something very liberating in owing no one, Mr Paterson. I made a very rash judgement in marrying Mr Fielding, and I have never regretted it, even for an hour. I have had some difficult times. I have been cold and hungry and very far from home, but I have never been bored or lonely, or felt as if my life had no meaning. I have lost certain friends – or perhaps in truth they were really no more than acquaintances – but I have gained friends who are of worth and I have contributed to doing something of value. I don't think I have ever been so happy before, even when I had very considerable money, social position and a very beautiful house. But then one person's happiness is not necessarily the same as another's.'

He lowered his eyes very slowly. 'I apologise, Mrs Fielding. I was extremely rude. I am afraid of losing what I know, and have always believed I wanted. I was afraid of Mr Ballin because he lured Alice away from me into another kind of world, but I did not kill him. I was with Lydia. If you ask her, I'm sure she will tell you.' He gave a rueful smile and met her eyes again. 'If I was with her, then she

133

was also with me. We were in the morning room until you went back up the stairs to your room to tell Mr Fielding about Ballin. I know that because we heard your footsteps and I looked out of the door to see who it was, so we could go upstairs unobserved. We had not realised how late it was, and we felt it would be indiscreet to be seen.'

'So it would,' she agreed. 'What was I wearing?'

'A . . . a pink dressing robe, and your hair was loose down your back. It is rather longer than it looks to be.'

She nodded slowly. 'It is fortunate you chose that particular moment to look. Thank you.'

'I . . . er . . .'

'You have no need to explain yourself further,' she told him. 'I shall confirm it with Lydia, and we shall be able to keep the police from bothering you – I hope.'

'Mrs Fielding . . .'

'Yes?'

'Thank you.'

She said nothing, but smiled a little bleakly and nodded.

It was after dark. The wind had dropped and the frost was bitter when Caroline spoke to the housemaid who usually changed her bed linen and tidied the room. She came in to give her clean towels, and after she had put them on the rail she stopped a moment, clearly wishing to speak. She was a handsome girl, but now her face was troubled. She kept moving her hands, rubbing one with the other as if the slight pain it must cause her were some kind of ease.

'What is it, Tess?' Caroline asked. She was almost certain what the girl was afraid of, and she sympathised with her.

'Is 'e ill wi' summat catching, ma'am?' she asked.

'No,' Caroline answered. She thought Eliza Netheridge might not forgive her, but the truth had to be told some time. 'I'm afraid Mr Ballin met with what may have been an accident, and he is dead. We did not tell you because we didn't wish everyone to be frightened, and to spoil Christmas.'

Tess's face flooded with relief, then she remembered the man was dead, and it was replaced with sorrow. ''E were a nice man, even if 'e were a bit odd, like. I'm sorry as 'e's dead, ma'am.'

'I think it happened very quickly.' Caroline tried to keep the imagination of it out of her mind, the violence, the pain and the blood, even if it had been brief. What she had seen would stay in her memory for ever. She hated this, but she would never have a better chance to speak to one of Netheridge's servants.

'The police are going to ask us what happened, because they have to know,' she went on. 'The poor man's family must be told.'

'I'm terrible sorry . . .'

'Of course. We all are. We are not quite sure what happened, and it would be better if we knew. Were you upstairs late in the evening?'

Tess nodded. 'I didn't stay. Mr Netheridge were . . . not 'isself.'

135

'He was ill?'

'No, ma'am, but 'e an' the mistress were 'avin' a disagreement . . .'

'What about?' Caroline did not make any excuses as to why she wanted to know. There were none that would not sound completely artificial. 'The play?'

'Oh, no, ma'am. It were about the drawin' room, an' such like, the dinin' room too. It'll all need redoin' pretty soon. Come the spring, at the latest. The master says it'll all be the same as 'is mam 'ad it. It always is. The mistress says as she'll 'ave it 'er own way this time, like she wants it. 'E says it's always been like 'is mam 'ad it, and she says it's time it was changed. They went on an' on like that, an' I know it wasn't no use askin' 'er anythin' about anythin' else that night, so I just went.'

'What time was that?'

'Just before midnight. I waited around, like, but it wasn't goin' to get any better, so I gave up.'

'How long do you think they argued?'

''Alf-hour, maybe more.'

'So you don't think they could have seen what happened to Mr Ballin?'

'No way, ma'am. They was too angry to see anythin' else but the curtains an' walls an' the like.'

'Were they going to redecorate the bedroom as well?'

'Yes, ma'am. An' the mistress says as it in't goin' to be brown this time.' She looked pleased. 'What lady, 'ceptin' 'is mam, wants a brown bedroom?'

'None,' Caroline agreed. 'Mine is mostly pink and red, and I love it.'

Tess breathed out in a sigh of pleasure. 'Cor! An' your 'usband don't mind?'

'If he did I wouldn't have done it. The pink is very pale and cool, and the red is hot. He likes it.'

Tess went out smiling so widely Caroline heard the other maid on the landing asking her what had happened. The tale of Caroline's bedroom would be all over the house in an hour; the knowledge of Ballin's death also.

The last person Caroline spoke to was Alice herself. She found her alone after dinner in a long gallery overlooking the snow-bound darkness of the countryside. There was nothing to see except an occasional light in the distance where the town lay, like them, shrouded in snow.

'I shall miss you when you're gone,' Alice said quietly. It was simply a statement. She did not seem to be expecting a reply. She took a deep breath. 'And I miss Mr Ballin. Do you think it was Douglas who killed him, Mrs Fielding?'

'No,' Caroline replied without hesitation. 'Nor was it your father.' She twisted around to face Alice. Even in the candle-light and shadow of the gallery, she could see the shock and the shame in the young woman's face.

'Were you not afraid of that too?' Caroline asked her. 'If you want to break off your engagement to Douglas and come to London, it will take a great change of heart in your father to allow that.' She bit her lip. 'And he might be a good deal less inclined to back our company in the future, if he feels we have influenced you towards that.'

'But he invited you up here to help me!' Alice protested. 'You came. If he then blamed you for what happened as a result that would be monstrously unfair.'

'Not really. He has no obligation to back us!'

'Isn't that why you came?'

Caroline felt the heat in her own face. It would be a lot less than honest to deny it. 'Yes. But things don't always work out the way you wish.'

'I have enough money to live for quite a while in London, before I earned anything.' Alice turned back to stare out of the window into the darkness.

'It would be a very big change,' Caroline warned.

'I know. Leaving home always is, but there are all sorts of ways in which I am not really at home here. I . . . I feel that if I marry Douglas I shall have stopped growing, the way a plant does if you put it in too small a pot. There'll be flowers that never open, fruit that never form.' She looked at Caroline again. 'Is it worth dying a little inside, just to be safe from hurt, or failure? And there's more than one kind of loneliness. You could spend all your life with people who know what they think you are, what they think you ought to be, and never let you be anything different.'

'Growing can hurt, and you don't always get what you want,' Caroline warned. 'Or sometimes you do, and then find you don't want it so much after all.'

'Is it better not to even try?' Alice asked earnestly. 'I was going to say "to stay at home", but surely "home" is where you are yourself, your best self, isn't it? I don't think that, for me, that is Whitby.'

'Then perhaps you had better find out,' Caroline conceded.

'Will you ask Mr Fielding to consider allowing me to join your group? I won't expect anything beyond the opportunity to work. And I won't ask to come with you now. That would be embarrassing for you, after this.'

'Of course I'll speak to him,' Caroline said quickly. 'I think if it is really what you want, then we will find a way to make it possible. But all the same, give it a little longer.'

Alice smiled. 'And I think maybe Miss Rye would be better for Douglas anyway. Haven't you noticed?'

'Yes, of course I have.'

'And I don't mind,' Alice said with surprise. 'When I realised that, then I knew I shouldn't marry him. It would be dishonest, and I don't want to start out lying to myself.'

'I don't see that possibility in you,' Caroline said frankly.

They all retired early. There was little to stay up for. It did not seem possible that it was Christmas Eve. Everything was motionless in the icy grip of the snow. No one had the heart to put up wreaths of holly or ivy, ribbons in scarlet, or any of the other usual ornaments. The weather had prevented the delivery of the tree they had planned. It would be a sombre Christmas, shorn of all the trimmings. Ballin's death haunted the minds of all of them.

Caroline lay in the dark wondering what else she could

do. They did not know when the thaw would come, but it could be within the next few days. Then the police would be sent for. The reality of murder would no longer be avoidable. The players would be suspected and every tragic or grubby secret would be dragged out, examined and very probably misunderstood. Unless she could find some answer before then.

Eliza had questioned the servants and they were all accounted for, as Caroline had expected. Joshua and Mr Netheridge had searched the house again, but they had still not found the body of Ballin. Where had they not looked? Why had anyone moved it? It could only be because there was something about it that would reveal who had killed him, and perhaps why.

Caroline stared up at the ceiling. She thought Joshua was asleep, but she was not yet certain. When she was, she already knew that she would get up and begin her own search. The answer was with Ballin himself.

But what form could the evidence possibly take? If it were paper, why not simply destroy it? That would be infinitely safer and simpler than moving the body. Ballin was quite a big man, and strong; he must be heavy. Inert bodies were not called 'dead weight' for nothing. No woman could have carried him alone. Two together would have found it difficult, but perhaps not impossible. One man might have managed, if he were strong and used to lifting.

Joshua was asleep. She was sure of it now. Very carefully she slid out of the bed and crept to the dressing room, feeling her way. Thank goodness they had a separate room for clothes where she could light a candle and dress without wakening him. She must dress warmly, even with boots. She might need to go somewhere unheated.

She considered going to the attics, but they were mostly servants' quarters. No doubt all the rooms would be used, one way or another, and the whole area would be far from private. Also who would willingly carry a dead body up four flights of stairs? There were the boxrooms up there, she knew, full of old furniture and suitcases, cabin trunks and the like. Excellent places to hide a body, but not if you were trying to do it alone, in the middle of the night.

She stood on the silent landing in the very faint candle-light, thinking. She must make no sound, or she would disturb someone. She could imagine the furore: the screaming if it were Mercy, or even Lydia; the outrage and suspicion if it were Mr Netheridge; the sarcasm if it were Vincent, or even James.

Of course one of them knew exactly where Ballin was. That was a thought she refused to entertain. It would paralyse her. Courage. She must use all the courage she had. And for heaven's sake, also the sense.

Don't be squeamish. How long did it take for a dead body to begin to rot, and to attract scavengers, not to mention to smell? The rats and flies, so loved of Renfield, would soon give away a corpse kept in a warm place. Therefore it would be hidden somewhere as cold as possible.

They burned both wood and coal in the house fires, so

141

there would be a coal cellar. Very possibly there would also be a place inside for wood, certainly at least for kindling. Had they looked there, thoroughly?

The ice house where the meat was kept, and other perishable food, would be perfect, but the servants would go in there regularly. They would even check all the stores to make sure nothing was spoiling. Though not the ice house.

She went down to the cloakroom where she had left her outside coat when she had arrived, not knowing then that they would be unable to take walks. She put on her boots also. The cellar would be bitterly cold, and dirty.

She lit one of the lanterns that were there in case someone needed to go outside, and set out to find the wood and coal cellar, and any other cold or disused room there might be for storing unneeded household articles too heavy to put in the attics.

An hour later she was aching, filthy, shuddering with cold, and she had found nothing that helped in the slightest to know what had happened to the body of Anton Ballin.

Think! It had to be somewhere. Was it conceivable that whoever had murdered him had somehow destroyed his corpse? How? Burning? The only possible place for a fire big enough to get a whole body into would be the furnace to heat the water in the laundry room. And the maids did the laundry regularly.

Were the fires kept going all night? Hardly likely, at least not hotly enough to destroy a corpse.

Still, she would look.

She went slowly, very reluctantly, to the laundry room. The fire under the big copper in which the sheets were boiled was glowing dimly. One might have burned a rat in it, but nothing bigger. And the smell would have been awful.

She stood in the middle of the room and turned around slowly. Apart from the copper there were deep tubs next to the wall, and mangles. On the shelves above, there were many jars for all kinds of substances: soaps, lye, starch, bottles of chemicals for cleaning various stains on different kinds of fabrics.

She walked slowly through to the drying room. Long airing racks were suspended from the ceiling to deal with the washing on days when it was impossible to dry anything outside.

There was another large tub by the wall. Caroline tiptoed over to it and lifted the lid, her heart pounding. There was nothing inside it but loose, light brown bran. It was useful for lifting certain stains, or for rubbing fabrics that needed extra care. Determined not to have to come back and do it again, if she missed it now, she found a wooden spoon with a long handle and poked it down into the bran. It met no resistance. With a gulp of relief she closed the lid.

There was nowhere else left to look, except the stillroom. There were plenty of bottles and jars, but a glance told her there was nowhere large enough for a corpse.

So where was he? It must be two in the morning and actually Christmas Day. And here she was, frozen cold, hunting around her hosts' kitchens for the body of a dead

143

man. And she had told Alice that life in a company of touring actors was fun!

The only place left was the ice house. It couldn't be there, but where else was there to look? The stables? No, Caroline knew enough of horses to rule that out. Horses smell death and are afraid of it. They would certainly let people know if there were any sort of death in the stables. Even in the hay loft the body would smell appalling, and they would have a plague of rats within hours, let alone days.

There was nothing for it but to go outside across the yard to the ice house. She went to the scullery door and unlocked it. Why anyone had bothered with the bolts in this weather was beyond her. Habit, and obedience possibly. They were stiff to move, and the top one was high, but she managed, with rather a noise. She hoped fervently that everyone else was asleep.

She pulled the door open and stepped out, holding the lantern high. She did not completely close the door: she needed the crack of light to guide her back, and somehow leaving it ajar did not seem so final.

The air was bitter but there was no wind at all. In fact, it was possible to imagine that it could thaw, just a little bit, by morning. She walked half a dozen steps across the yard. The snow was completely untrodden since yesterday's fall and there was not a mark on it. It was deep enough to cover the top of her boots and cling to her skirts. When it melted she would be soaked.

The ice house was ahead of her, half under some trees

whose black branches seemed to rest on the roof. There was something else up there: piles of wood like discarded floor-boards, or something of the sort, half-covered with snow. There were more timbers to one side, and bags of something. Coal? No, there was room in the cellar. Kindling? It would get soaked and be no use. Perhaps rubbish no one had been able to dispose of properly in the snow.

In spite of the stillness, the wind seemed to sigh a little in the bare branches, and several lumps of snow fell off. She was right: it was thawing, just a tiny bit.

Could they have put his body out here, with the rubbish? How long could it remain hidden? Perhaps they planned to do something else with it then?

She walked with difficulty, having to lift her feet unnaturally high in the deep snow where it had drifted. Should she look now, or ask Joshua to help her in daylight? What a cowardly thing to do, when she didn't even know if there were anything here or not. And maybe if whoever killed Ballin saw the footsteps in the snow leading to the side of the ice house, they would know someone had been there, and move the body anyway.

She reached the sacks of rubbish, holding the lantern high so she could see. The timber had slid a little and several pieces were lying over the tops of the bags. She put the lantern down carefully and started to lift the top piece of wood. She put it to one side and lifted the next one.

Then it happened – the shift in the snow on the roof. She looked up. A few lumps dropped off and fell onto the sacks.

The stars were brilliant above the pale outline of the ridge, and she could see the ends of wood poking up. A larger lump of snow fell. Then as she stepped back, without thinking, pulling the wood with her, there was a roar of sliding snow on the slates. A figure launched itself at her, diving downwards, head thrown back, mouth wide open. It struck her so hard she staggered backwards, falling into the deep snow as it landed hard on top of her. By the yellow light of the lantern she saw the hideously distorted face, glaring eyes, flesh eaten away and sliding off, teeth bared.

She screamed, again and again, her lungs aching.

Nothing happened. No one came.

Ballin's terrible face was inches from her, his body hard as rock. But something had happened to it, beyond agony, beyond death. The flesh of his cheeks seemed to have half dissolved and slipped sideways, crookedly. Even his nose was rotted away, twisted to one side.

For a moment she thought her heart was going to burst. She was alone in the night with the face of evil, the vampire without his human mask. This thing was a creature of the night, dead and yet not dead.

There was no one to help. She must do this alone. She steadied her breath and forced herself to lift the lantern a little, and look at it. It was frozen rigid, as unbending as the planks of wood that had held it up there on the ice house roof.

His face was terrible, as if it were falling apart. How could that happen in the paralysing cold, and so soon after death?

She made herself look at it again, steadily. Her hand shook and the light of the lantern wavered over Ballin's face. Caroline stared at it and slowly she realised that it was not decay that made him look as if he were rotting and falling apart. His face was literally sliding off his skin. It was an actor's make-up. More than greasepaint, he had a thin layer of some rubbery kind of substance, a gum of some nature, to pad out his cheeks and nose. Underneath it she saw the harder, deeper lines of a different face, one that in some half-remembered way was vaguely familiar. She knew him, but she had no idea from where, or when.

And as she understood that, she knew why his killer had moved the body.

Very slowly, shuddering with cold and horror, she pushed him away and stood up. She must go and tell Joshua. If nothing else, they must put the body in some decent place, not leave him lying on the ground by the ice house. None of the servants, rising early to prepare breakfast, must find him.

She tramped back through the snow to the back door. Thank heaven it was still slightly ajar. Her teeth were chattering with the cold. She went inside and closed the door.

She walked slowly through the scullery into the kitchen. She was trailing water behind her. Her whole coat was covered with snow from when she had fallen, and her skirt was wet for at least a foot above the hem, or more.

Where had she seen Ballin's face before? It was in a photograph, she was sure of that, not the man in person.

147

His name had not been Ballin. She would have remembered that. Anton. Had it been Anton something else?

She was in the hallway now. Only a couple of lamps were alight. The tall clock said it was nearly three in the morning. She reached the bottom of the stairs and started up, holding her soaked skirt high so as not to trip over it.

She was almost at the landing when she remembered. It was a photograph in the green room of a theatre: Joshua had pointed it out to her because he saw the man as a great actor. Anton Rausch. A handsome face, powerful. A tragedy connected to it. He had killed some actress in a murder scene in a play. A knife. It was supposed to have been a stage prop whose blade would retract when it met resistance. Only it had not done. He had replaced it with a real knife.

Or someone had.

It had ruined his career.

Caroline realised she was standing still at the top of the stairs. The cold ate through the fabric of her clothes and chilled her flesh.

She walked to her own bedroom and opened the door. She still had the lantern and she set it down on the dresser.

'Joshua,' she said calmly.

He stirred.

'Joshua. I know who killed Ballin, and why. I found his body.'

He sat up, fighting the remnants of sleep. Then he saw her clearly. 'Caroline! What happened?' He started to climb out of bed.

'It's all right,' she said, her voice perfectly steady. 'I'm cold, and a bit wet, but I'm perfectly all right. I found Ballin's body.'

'Where?' He was up now. He reached for his robe, warm and dry, and put it around her. 'Did you say you know who killed him, or was I imagining it?'

'Anton Rausch,' she said quietly. She was shivering uncontrollably now.

'Ballin?' he said incredulously. 'Oh God! Of course. I should have known the voice. I saw him play Hamlet! I only met him in person once. Oh heaven, I see.'

'Do you?' she asked.

'Yes. Vincent. He was the other actor involved, the lover of the actress,' he answered. 'Anton Rausch was her husband.'

'Then Ballin came here for revenge? How could he know Vincent was here? And why now? That was years ago.'

'Perhaps Anton could prove his innocence now. I don't know.'

'But if he attacked Vincent, for revenge, then Vincent is not guilty of murder. It doesn't make a lot of sense,' she argued. 'And how did he know Vincent was here?'

Joshua shook his head. 'It wasn't a secret. The theatre knew where we would be, the manager, the people who had to. It just wasn't advertised because it was a private performance.'

'But Ballin attacked him – I still think of him as Ballin. Why didn't Vincent defend himself?' she repeated.

'Because Anton didn't attack him,' Joshua said quietly. 'Think about it, Caroline. If Anton had attacked Vincent with

149

that sharpened broom handle then Vincent would have injuries: tears on his skin at least, wrenched muscles where they fought, bruises, perhaps rips in his clothes. It was one lethal blow in the chest. Vincent attacked Anton and took him by surprise. He went armed. He intended to kill Anton before Anton could prove who actually changed the knives.'

She tried to imagine it. 'How could he prove that, after all this time?'

'I don't know. Perhaps someone's dying confession. A stage hand, a prop man. We'll never know now.'

'Then why didn't he just tell the authorities, and have Vincent arrested?'

'I don't know. Lots of possibilities. Perhaps he wanted Vincent to do something for him, a repayment other than answer to the law.'

'Poor man,' she said quietly. 'We can't leave him lying in the snow by the ice house. Should we waken Mr Netheridge and tell him?'

'Yes. I think so. Since this is his house, he deserves to know. We have taken enough liberties already.'

'Have we?'

He smiled. 'Yes. Very definitely. And unfortunately we won't even be entertaining his guests on Boxing Day.'

'But you will help Alice, won't you?'

'Of course. We might even perform *Dracula* sometime.' He smiled with a wry twist, his eyes gentle. 'But we will have to find another Van Helsing.'

* * *

In the morning, breakfast was eaten, largely in silence. Then Mr Netheridge asked the other guests to leave the with-drawing room for a certain matter of business he had to attend to, and asked Joshua, Caroline and Vincent Singer to join him there. Perhaps no one except Caroline noticed that the butler and three footmen were waiting in the hall.

'Is this about Alice . . . Miss Netheridge?' Vincent asked curiously when the doors were closed.

'No,' Netheridge replied. 'I think perhaps Mr Fielding will explain it best.'

Vincent was standing in front of the great stained-glass window. His back was to the magnificent view it partially concealed, even though it was possible to see, through its paler sections, the sunlight on the snow beyond.

'How melodramatic,' he said, looking at Caroline. 'You seem to have acquired a taste for acting yourself. It needs a lot more practice. Your timing is poor, and timing is everything.'

'Actually I prefer the writing side of it, and the work with the lights,' she responded. 'So much depends on which light you see things in. Anton Rausch taught me that,' she replied.

Vincent paled. Suddenly his body was stiff, his hands clenched.

'I found his body,' she added simply. She touched her own cheek. 'The make-up had slipped, and I recognised him from a photograph I saw in a theatre. He was a great actor, better than you, Vincent. That's what it was all about, wasn't it? Nothing to do with the actress, beautiful as she was.'

Vincent's face hardened. 'He came for revenge. He didn't know who it was at the time it happened, and of course they gaoled him. He must have worked it out, or somebody else did and told him. He attacked me. He came at me with that broom handle, spiked at the end like the blade of a halberd.' He lifted his shoulder a little, his gaze steady on her face. 'Wicked-looking thing. I barely had time to defend myself and turn his lunge back against him.'

'Vincent, don't make more of a fool of yourself than necessary,' Joshua said wearily. 'You are at the end of this. There is no way you could have turned a weapon that length against the man holding it. And there are no wounds on you. You attacked him, to protect yourself from the truth coming out. I'm sure he did want revenge, at a price you could not afford.'

It was Netheridge who moved towards him. 'The snow is thawing. We'll be able to get a man out to fetch the police by tomorrow. Until then we'll lock you in one of the storerooms . . .'

Vincent sprang suddenly and without any warning. He leaped forward and grasped a light wooden chair. If he smashed it then one of its legs would make a dagger of hard, sharp-pointed wood. But Caroline picked up the onyx ashtray from the table nearest her and threw it at him. He ducked it, caught his arm in the huge velvet curtain and lost his balance. He fell backwards, dragging the curtain with him, fighting hard and panicking. There was a splintering crash and the whole vast stained-glass window buckled and flew outwards, Vincent with it. His thin scream echoed back in the air, and then stopped.

Caroline felt the sudden rush of cold air, and at the same moment heard in the silence the church bells in the distance ringing out Christmas morning in Whitby.

Slowly she walked over to the gaping space and stared down, forcing herself to look. Vincent lay on his back on the paved forecourt two storeys beneath, arms and legs splayed like a broken doll in the snow.

She heard movement and felt Joshua's arm around her, holding her tightly, close to him.

'There's nothing you can do,' he said, his voice catching a little. 'I'd rather it were this way, for Vincent as well as for us.'

'I suppose it is better,' she agreed. She turned back from the clean, icy air towards the room again.

Eliza had come in and was staring at the remnants of the window, her face ashen.

'I'm sorry,' Caroline apologised.

Netheridge cleared his throat and put his arm around Eliza. 'Not your fault, Mrs Fielding. It was a tragedy that just happened to end here. Mr Singer let the evil in a long time ago. I've learned a thing or two from your play, bits I've seen, an' Eliza's told me about. Time to let the good in too. Kept too many doors shut for too long.'

Caroline nodded very slowly, and smiled at him.

'At least it is now over. We shall never forget what happened to poor Mr Ballin here this Christmas; but somehow we must move forward with our lives.'

'Too true,' said Netheridge 'Now, though, the snow is melting and it is time to contact the police. Later, let us try and enjoy the remainder of this Christmas period.'

Behind them, the church bells joined in, as if in welcome of the day to come, when briefly all mankind is at home and peace comes to the world.

Headline hopes you have enjoyed reading Anne Perry's *A Christmas Homecoming*, and invites you to read a sample of *A Christmas Garland*, which is out now.

Lieutenant Victor Narraway walked across the square in the cool evening air. It was mid-December, a couple of weeks before Christmas. At home in England it might already be snowing, but here in India there would not even be a frost. No one had ever seen snow in Cawnpore. Any other year it would be a wonderful season: one of rejoicing, happy memories of the past, optimism for the future, perhaps a little nostalgia for those one loved who were far away.

But this year of 1857 was different. The fire of mutiny had scorched across the land, touching everything with death.

He came to the outer door of one of the least-damaged parts of the barracks and knocked. Immediately it was opened and he stepped inside. Oil lamps sent a warming yellow light over the battered walls and the few remnants of the once secure occupation, before the siege and then its relief a few months ago. There was little furniture left whole: a bullet-scarred desk, three chairs that had seen better days, a bookcase and several cupboards, one with only half a door.

Colonel Latimer was a tall and spare man well into his forties. A dozen Indian summers had burned his skin brown, but there was little colour beneath it to give life to the weariness and the marks of exhaustion. He regarded the twenty-year-old lieutenant in front of him with something like apology.

'I have an unpleasant duty for you, Narraway,' he said quietly. 'It must be done, and done well. You're new to this regiment, but you have an excellent record. You are the right man for this job.'

Narraway felt a chill, in spite of the mildness of the air. His father had purchased a commission for him and he had served a brief training in England before being sent out to India. He had arrived a year ago, just before the issue of the fateful cartridges at Dum Dum in January, which later in the spring had erupted in mutiny. The rumour had been that they were covered in animal grease in the part required to be bitten in order to open them for use. The Hindus had been told it was beef fat. Cows were sacred and to kill one was blasphemy. To put the fat to the lips was damnation. The Muslims had been told it was pork fat, and the pig was an unclean animal. To put that grease to your lips would damn your soul, although for an entirely different reason.

Of course, that was not the cause of the mutiny by hundreds of thousands of Indians against the rule of a few thousand Englishmen employed by the East India Company. The real reasons were more complex, far more deeply rooted in the social inequities and the cultural offences of a foreign rule. This was merely the spark that had ignited the fire.

Also it was true, as far as Narraway could gather, that the mutiny was far from universal. It was violent and terrible only in small parts of the country. Thousands of miles were untouched by it, lying peaceful, if a little uneasy, under the winter sun.

But the province of Sind on the Hindustan plains had seen much of the very worst of it, Cawnpore and Lucknow in particular.

General Colin Campbell, a hero from the recent war in the Crimea, had fought his way through to relieve the siege at Lucknow. A week ago he had defeated 25,000 rebels here at Cawnpore. Was it the beginning of a turning in the tide? Or just a glimmer of light that would not last?

Narraway stood to attention, breathing deeply to calm himself. Why had he come to Latimer's notice?

'Yes, sir,' he said between his teeth.

Latimer smiled bleakly. There was no light in his face, no warmth of approval. 'You will be aware of the recent escape of the prisoner Dhuleep Singh,' he went on. 'And that in order to achieve it the guard Chuttur Singh was hacked to death.'

Narraway's mouth was dry. Of course he knew it; everyone in the Cawnpore station knew it.

'Yes, sir,' he said obediently, forcing the words out.

'It has been investigated.' Latimer's jaw was tight; a small muscle jumped in his temple. 'Dhuleep Singh had privileged information regarding troop movements, specifically the recent patrol that was massacred. The man could not have escaped without assistance.' His voice was growing quieter, as if he found the words more and more difficult to say. He cleared his throat with an effort. 'Our enquiries have excluded every possibility, except that he was helped by Corporal John Tallis, the medical orderly.' He met Narraway's eyes. 'We will try him the day after tomorrow. I require you to speak in his defence.'

Narraway's mind whirled. There was a chill like ice in the pit of his stomach. A score of reasons leaped to his mind why he could not do what Latimer was asking of him. He was not even remotely equal to the task. It would be so much better to have one of the officers who had been with the regiment during the siege and the relief, and who knew everyone. Above all, they should have an officer who was experienced in military law, who had done this dozens of times, and was known and respected by the men.

Then a cold, sane voice inside assured him that it was precisely because he was none of these things that Latimer had chosen him.

'Yes, sir,' he said faintly.

'Major Strafford will be here any moment,' Latimer continued. 'He will give you any instruction and advice that you may need. I shall be presiding over the court, so it is not appropriate that I should do it.'

'Yes, sir,' Narraway said again, feeling as if another nail had been driven into the coffin lid of his career. Major

Strafford's dislike of him dated from before the time he had joined the regiment. Almost certainly it came from Narraway's brief acquaintance with Strafford's younger brother. They had been in the same final year at Eton, and little about their association had been happy.

Narraway had been academic, a natural scholar and disinclined towards sports. The younger Strafford was a fine athlete, but no competition for Narraway in the classroom. They existed happily enough in a mutual contempt. It was shattered one summer evening in a magnificent cricket match, nail-bitingly close but Strafford's team having the edge, until Narraway showed a rare flash of brilliance in the only sport he actually enjoyed. The dark, slender scholar, without a word spoken, bowled out the last three men in Strafford's team, including the great sportsman himself. The fact that he did it with apparent ease was appalling, but that he did not overtly take any pleasure in it was unforgivable.

Strafford Minor had never been able to exact his revenge in the field, which was the only place where he could redeem his honour. Other quarrels or victories did not count. No practical joke or barbed wit looked anything better than the spite of a bad loser.

But that was boyhood, two years ago and thousands of miles away.

'Captain Busby will prosecute,' Latimer was going on. 'The evidence seems simple enough. You will be free to interview Corporal Tallis at any time you wish, and anyone else you feel could be helpful to your defence. Any legal points that you need clarifying, speak to Major Strafford.'

'Yes, sir.' Narraway was still at attention, his muscles aching with the effort of keeping complete control of himself.

There was a brief knock on the door.

'Come,' Latimer ordered.

The door swung open and Major Strafford came in. He was a tall, handsome man in his early thirties, but the echo of Narraway's schoolfellow, so much his junior, was there in the set of his shoulders, the thick, fair hair, the shape of his jaw.

Strafford glanced at Latimer.

'Sir.' He saluted, then, as he was given permission, relaxed. He regarded Narraway expressionlessly. 'You'd better read up on it tonight and start questioning people tomorrow morning,' he said. 'You need to be sure of the law. We don't want anyone afterwards saying that we cut corners. I presume you appreciate that?'

'Yes, sir.' Narraway heard the edge of condescension in Strafford's voice and would dearly like to have told him that he was as aware as anyone else of how they would all be judged on their conduct in the matter. More than that, the future of British rule in India would be flavoured by report of decisions such as this. The whole structure of Empire hung together on the belief in justice, in doing things by immutable rules and a code of honour that they themselves never broke.

Thousands of men were dead already, as well as women and children. If they ever regained control and there were to be any kind of peace, it must be under the rule of law. It was the only safety for people of any colour or faith. Once they themselves gave in to barbarism there was no hope left for anyone. Right now, there seemed to be little enough in any circumstances. Delhi had fallen, Lucknow, Agra, Jhelum, Sugauli, Dinapoor, Lahore, Kolapore, Ramgarh, Peshawar – and on and on. The list seemed endless. Perhaps there was nothing left but some shred of honour.

'Good,' Strafford said curtly. 'Whatever you think you know, you'd better come and see me and tell me at least the outline of your defence.' He looked at Narraway closely, his blue eyes curiously luminous in the light of the oil lamp. 'You must be sure to mount some defence, you do understand that, don't you? At least put forward a reason why a man like Tallis should betray the men he's served beside all his career. I know he's quarter Indian, or something of the sort, but that's no excuse.'

The tight muscles in his face twitched. 'For God's sake, thousands of soldiers are still loyal to their regiments and to the Crown, and fighting on our side. Tens of thousands more are going about their duties as usual. No one knows what the end of this will be. Find out what the devil got into the man. Threats, bribery, drunk and lost his wits? Give some explanation.'

Narraway felt dismay turn to anger. It was bad enough

that he was picked out to defend the indefensible; now Strafford required him to explain it as well.

'If Corporal Tallis has an explanation, sir, I shall offer it,' he replied in a hard, controlled voice. 'I cannot imagine one that will excuse his conduct, so it will be brief.'

'The explanation is not to excuse him, Lieutenant,' Strafford said acidly. 'It is to help the garrison here feel as if there is some sense in the world, some tiny thread of reason to hold on to, when everything they know has turned into chaos and half the people we loved are slaughtered like animals, and the nation on every side is in ruins.' A flush spread up his fair face, visible even in this wavering light. 'You are here to satisfy the law so that we do not appear to history to have betrayed ourselves and all we believe in, not to excuse the damned man! I know you are new here, but you must have at least that much sense!'

'Strafford . . .' Latimer said quietly, interrupting for the first time. 'We have given the lieutenant a thankless task, and he is quite aware of it. If he isn't now, he will be when he has looked at it a trifle more closely.' He turned to Narraway again. 'Lieutenant, we do not know where we shall be by the turn of the year, here or somewhere else, besieged or comparatively free. This matter must be dealt with before then. The women and children need a celebration, however meagre. We need hope, and we cannot have that without a quiet conscience. We cannot celebrate the birth of the Son of God, nor can we ask His help with confidence, if we do so with dishonour weighing us down. I expect you to conduct Tallis's defence in such a manner that we have no stain on our conduct to cripple us in the future. Do I make myself clear?'

Narraway took a deep breath and let it out slowly. 'Yes, sir,' he said as if he had some idea in his head how to do it. It was a lie, by implication, as he saluted and left the room. He had no idea whatever.

He walked away from the command building across the dry earth without any notion of where he was going. It was totally dark now, and the sky was burning with stars and a low, three-quarter moon. There was sufficient light to see the broken outline of the walls and the black billows of the tamarind trees, motionless in the still air. His feet made no sound on the dry earth.

He passed few other people, even on the road beyond the intrenchment. Sentries took no notice of him. In his uniform he passed unquestioned.

Half a mile away the vast Ganges River murmured and shifted in the moonlight, reflecting an almost unbroken surface, only streaked here and there where the current eddied.

The prisoner who had escaped and the guard he had so savagely murdered were both Sikhs. That in itself was not extraordinary. The Sikhs had been on either side during the mutiny. India was made up of many races and religions, languages and variations in culture from region to region. Petty wars and squabbles abounded.

John Tallis was British, but one of his grandparents had

been Indian – Narraway had no idea from where, or even if they had been Hindu, Sikh, Jain, Muslim or something else. He dreaded meeting the man: yet, as soon as he had any clarity in his mind as to how he should approach the subject, he must do it.

The crime had been monstrous and there could be no defence. The guard, Chuttur Singh, had been hacked to death. It had not been even a simple breaking of the neck, or cutting his throat, which, while gruesome, would at least have been quick. The massacre of the patrol was equally bloody, but it was, in a sense, part of war and so to be expected. But it would not have happened had the enemy now known exactly where to find them, and at what hour.

What had changed John Tallis from a first-class medical aide of compassion and loyalty into a man who could betray his own?

Narraway was walking slowly, but already he was on the beginning of the street that led into the battered and bedrag-gled town. In the distance he could see the spires of two of the churches against the skyline. Nearer him there were a couple of shops with their doors closed. There was hardly anyone around, just a glimpse of light visible here and there from a half-shuttered window, a sound of laughter, a woman singing, the smell of food. The air was chilling rapidly with the darkness. If he stood still he would become aware of the cold.

He started to walk again, smelling the dampness of the

river as he came closer to it. The earth was softer under his feet.

What did Latimer really expect of him? He had implied that he required Narraway to find something that made sense of Tallis's act. People needed to understand. No one can fight chaos. Maybe unreason is the last and worst fear, the one against which we have no weapons?

Was Latimer, as the man in command, the one everybody looked towards, trying to create a belief in order, a reason to fight?

Narraway came through the last trees and stared across the surging water, away to the north-east where he knew Lucknow was, beyond the horizon. Exactly a month before Christmas, General Havelock had died outside the city, worn out, beaten and bereaved. Had he finally seen the consuming darkness of loss and panic, and been overwhelmed by it, unable to see hope?

How much morale is affected by the character of a leader? It was a lesson Narraway had been taught over and over again, both at school and, later, in his military training. An officer must know his tactics, must understand both his own men and his enemy, must be familiar with the terrain and with the weapons, must guard his supply lines, must gain all the intelligence of the enemy that he possibly can. Above all he must earn the trust and the love of his men. He must act decisively and with honour, knowing what he is fighting for and believing in its worth.

Latimer had to deal with John Tallis immediately, and in

such a way that no one afterwards would look back on it with shame. They needed that for their own survival.

Victor Narraway had been chosen to bear the burden of defending a man totally indefensible. He was strategically and emotionally trapped, exactly as if he were besieged himself in the city of his own duty, and there was no escape, no relief column coming.

It was already late. There was no point in waiting any longer. The situation would not get better. He turned away from the sheet of light on the river and walked into the shadows again, making his way back towards the barracks and the makeshift prison where John Tallis was being kept until his trial, and inevitable sentence to death.

He must begin tonight.